# Breakfast at Midnight

## Louis Armand

# Breakfast at Midnight

LOUIS ARMAND

EQUUS

© Louis Armand, 2012
Cover image: Libor Fára, *Rezonance jejího večera* / z cyklu *Snídaně o půlnoci* / 1950
© the Estate of Libor Fára & the National Gallery, Prague

ISBN 978-0-9571213-0-0

Equus Press
Birkbeck College (William Rowe), 43 Gordon Square, London, WC1 H0PD, United Kingdom

Typeset by lazarus
Printed in the Czech Republic by PB Tisk

# BREAKFAST AT MIDNIGHT

| | |
|---|---|
| 1. ALL BLACKNESS TURNING GREY | 9 |
| 2. RESURRECTION | 14 |
| 3. ORIENT EXPRESS | 20 |
| 4. SLIP KNOT | 25 |
| 5. FETISH MACHINE | 32 |
| 6. ULTRAVIOLET | 41 |
| 7. FIESTA PIG | 48 |
| 8. ACE OF SPADES | 54 |
| 9. ST PAULI | 59 |
| 10. NUESTRA SEÑORA DE LA PAZ | 66 |
| 11. TEMPLE OF LOST SOULS | 74 |
| 12. RIOJA | 81 |
| 13. LA FIN DU MONDE | 86 |
| 14. PROVIDENCE | 94 |
| 15. SOLITAIRE | 100 |
| 16. SNAKE HOUSE | 107 |
| 17. CELLULOID | 113 |
| 18. REALISM | 121 |
| 19. WIND BECOMES WATER | 127 |
| 20. MANDALA | 134 |
| 21. MONKEY'S MOON | 140 |
| 22. ACCORDION | 145 |
| 23. CAMERA EYE | 151 |
| 24. TRÓJA | 158 |

*i.m. A.R.R*
*agent of Blakean apocalypse*

Notre jeunesse, c'étaient des cadavres faits pour danser, qu'à tout moment la vie pouvait distraire de cette joie.

*– Montaigne*

La vérité est trop nue; elle n'excite pas les hommes.

*– Cocteau*

# 1

## ALL BLACKNESS TURNING GREY

Another four a.m. struggling to make the demons shut up. An erratic light stutters overhead. Through the porthole, a dark blanket of mist & drizzle. Black water streaks the glass. Somewhere in the night a freight train sheers off the last threads of sleep, a banshee's screech phasing out into shortwave radio hiss.

Regen used to say, when we dream that we dream, we're beginning to wake up. Am I dreaming then? I lie there like someone who's died with their eyes open. Everything shudders into focus in a kind of aftershock. It's been like this since she left. I wake up & all I can remember is blackness, the sound of bees, a face staring up at me with eyes full of blood.

It's cold. There's a woman's voice in the distance, echo of laughter, static & white noise. Then I wake again. And it's the same.

♠

It's always the same, the face inside the dream. Those eyes. *Don't look at the eyes.* A fit of coughing wracks me & the image turns to red. Jag upright. There's a sound of breaking glass, debris. Empty bottles litter the floor. Been sleeping in my clothes again. Old undertaker's suit, Gestapo coat. Gradually the coughing subsides. I imagine struggling on the edge of a precipice, boots dangling, vertigo. The fall into space, the recoil. Something snaps underfoot, the way something snaps in your life. A muffled sound in the shadows. The alarm clock blinking thirteen minutes past four. Squint, waiting for thirteen to become fourteen, but the numbers don't change. Nowhere-time.

I make it as far as the sink before everything upends. Taste of gunmetal, stomach acid, diesel. I keep heaving but nothing comes out. Pain behind the eyes – staring too hard, trying to force shapes together, hold them in place. Down below, the Styx-grey waters, groaning against the hull, the groans of the damned. Faces down there, rippling with the tide. Dead souls.

When I look in the mirror it isn't pretty. A face like something left too long in water, hair matted with cold sweat. I wonder if I'm as ugly to others as I am to myself. Pull back, straining to breathe – grope down the companionway. There's nothing to drink in the galley but a carton of soured milk. I drink it anyway, to kill the acid taste. Reminds of damp bed sheets & soda bread. The way my mother used to curdle milk with lemon juice. Once upon a time, staring up at a plum tree with a white rope of bed linen hanging in it. A vertical line through the foliage & that same soured milk smell. Grass thick with rotten plums, ants, wasps, fruit flies swarming over them. Sound of bees. A pair of black leather high heel shoes covered in ants.

♠

I get lost sometimes, head filled with too much noise. In the half-dark, the galley's all unhinged – a puzzle-cube with pieces missing, other pieces sticking out at wrong angles. I let my eyes close, inhale slow & deep. The shortwave's hissing still. I reach through darkness & switch it off. Wait. Eyes open. Grey light settles on the floor, the table-top, crates of paper & refuse. All blackness turning grey.

Up on deck it's warmer than it was. Sign of a thaw setting in, post-rigor-mortis. The air's brewery-sour. A depthless mist hangs over the river, seeping up the riverbank – restless spirits seethe out of it. I stand at the bow breathing-in the alien atmosphere, arcing a stream of piss onto river ice.

Bird sounds echo from skeleton trees across the river. Sharp animal movements. Sentry codes. Night heron, heard, not seen – they sense dawn's relay, the slow heave of celestial gravity. I try to sense it too, dull psychic fingers groping outward, across its Braille. Thinking: *One wrong step.* Dark rivulets criss-cross the ice – runic scriptures threaded on gobs of fatuous light. Lines that run out where bodyweight falls off into nothingness. Some sixth sense urging you back from the edge, down the steel gangplank where flakes of rust graze your hands. Roped electrical cables weave the mist overhead, vine-like.

From the shore, everything immediately appears different. The barge hovers in the mist like a strip of wet tarmac. An old Spiller's barge that came down from Hamburg, before the great flood. Engine stripped out, fuel tanks & prop shaft. Antediluvian. Four letters of a name barely legible across the bow. G. O. R. A. This is my Ark on its moveable mountain. Six hundred tonnes of rivets & steel waiting to be scrapped.

A circle of light blinks at stern. Febrile Morse. Groping the fuse box I reset the fuses, back to zero. The light goes out & comes on again through the porthole window. Stilled now. Gibbous moon. The shortwave crackle starting up. A dog grunts from somewhere nearby, rattling its chain.

♠

Above the dry docks a path leads along the slipway to the rear of the container yard. Drizzle on junk-mounds & slagheaps. Empty warehouses loom in silhouette beside a demolition site. I pass the gatehouse, a lit square of window where the night watchman's sleeping in front of a TV. The TV's blue aquarium flicker. Sleepless mastiffs stalk the perimeter.

Across the street a taxi idles outside a nightclub called *St Pauli's*. The only thing that lets you know it's a claphouse is the strip of neon over the doorway. A gypsy with her skirt hiked around her waist is weaving a path up the stairs. *Fin-de-millénaire* Euro-trash drifts through the doorway. Voices, cracked, boozed up to the eyeballs. Canned laughter. A concertina of collapsed innards wheezing onto the pavement.

Inside, the air stinks of sweat & booze & expired perfume. A peroxide blonde is standing behind the bar with dark crescents for eyes. I need a drink, but the place has a sour used-up atmosphere where a drink's just a way-station on a downward run. A pit-bull in a burgundy polyester suit gives me the evil eye & I scowl back at him. There's a party of drunks holding up the walls, chewing the air with a couple of bored-looking whores. I ask for a coffee & the blonde pours something nasty into a cup. A soup of muddy grounds, Turkish-style. The caffeine jolts hard. I give the pit-bull another scowl & throw some change on the counter.

I'm back outside, circling around, following a random trajectory. Orange streetlights ooze through mist. Up ahead, a garbage truck is undoing the secret arrangements of trash along the sidewalks. The god of entropy in his heaven looking down. A night tram thuds past, headlights boring holes in the mist – grey faces behind fogged glass. Intermittent traffic out of the city's dark open-cut. I walk on with a sick animal alertness towards Libeňský Bridge. Somewhere the sound of a bell echoes over water. Clochecall. Siren. Cockcrow. The mist parts like a stage curtain. The river's dark sheen opens out, red & green navigation lights receding – the eye of the TV tower fucking down into it.

♠

The bridge has no end, telescoping into mist & fog, like a bridge in dreams. The rain starts up again, heavier now, wetting my face – collar pulled up around my ears. I realise I'm shivering, but not from the cold. It can't be far now. The pale orb of a clock face stuck above a graffitied tram shelter. Dead hands hanging down vertical. An electric billboard lies shattered on the ground, plumb lines of steel mesh keeping the shards together. Inside the shelter a bum's sprawled unconscious across a ruined steel bench, pockets turned-out – a body in a wrong arrangement beneath a sky full of broken glass. Headlights flare out of the gloom. The sound of footsteps. Laughter, like a swarm of bees, swarming closer.

I turn, but there's no-one. Jaws tense. The fog swarms with imagined adversaries – the click of a blade opening, slivers underfoot. Primal fear instincts. Something that crawled from Jurassic swamps, given body, flesh & blood. *Those eyes.*

A pair of yellowed orbs leer out of the night. I stare back at them, an animal too dumb to move. The great beast heaves like a mechanical leviathan with its springs winding down. Its mouths open. Foul breath warm & thick with old mastications. I give myself up to it. I'm surrendering. Actions without reason. The night tram pulls away. I let it take me to the end of the bridge & begin walking back again, going nowhere, killing time.

# 2
## RESURRECTION

It's just before seven when Blake wheels up on an old Enfield he swindled off a Sikh from Bombay. He's wearing a pair of WWII flying goggles & a greatcoat with a fox fur collar, like he's in some sort of movie – silver hair fanning up from the top of his head – unshaven – eyes a mess of broken capillaries. He gestures for me to get on behind him & I do. Like straddling a packhorse. Blake says something over his shoulder, but I can't hear it.

I was back below deck when he called, communing with lost spirits. Candles set out on a tin tray with crows' feet, bones of rat. A shrine to unholy powers. The galley's walls are covered with pictures cut from old magazines. Any sort of magazine you can imagine, scavenged from the dump sites on Libeňský Island. The cut-outs are all faces. Part of a puzzle, trying to pick up a trail, a scent, clues channelled by whatever means are at hand. The voodoo of discarded images, secret metamorphoses of the animal brain in its grief & mourning. If I look deep enough, perhaps all those faces can be made to reveal the one that isn't there, like an approximation of something that can't be grasped.

A face lost in the rain.

The first thing Blake said when I picked up the phone was that someone was dead. I was staring at the wall, trying to see through it backwards in time & place, to make all the images connect, when the words hit me. *Who's dead?* He said to meet him outside *St Pauli's* & hung up. I held onto the phone, waiting, but there was only static. *Who's dead?* I was sitting there in a second-hand undertaker's suit, the one I'd slept in.

Outside it'd stopped drizzling but it was the kind of grey that evokes funerals & cemeteries. I thought: *You'll look the part, at least.*

"YOU LOOK LIKE HELL." Blake, shouting this time so I can hear him over the engine. A two cylinder 500cc. I catch my reflection in the rearview. He's right. I look even worse than he does.

"WHERE ARE WE GOING?"

"TO PAY OUR LAST RESPECTS."

"AT THIS HOUR?"

It doesn't seem right. Waking the dead.

Blake shrugs, easing out the clutch. We pull into the early morning traffic & head for the bridge. Even without the rain there's slush & mud everywhere. The river's still curtained in mist. We ride across to the island & follow an exit ramp that winds down under the bridge, past junkyards & used car lots. From here the island stretches out into marsh & landfill – a place of illicit deals & contract killings. This is the Prague nobody wants to think about, saturated with dereliction, like an unconscious – sordid, grotesque. It would be easy to believe there's nothing here anyone would ever be nostalgic for. Piles of rubble loom out of the fog – the half-demolished silhouettes of warehouses, smashed walls, archaeologies of broken doorframes, bottle glass, enamelled runes.

The fog casts back the echo of engine-sounds eerily as the Enfield slaloms along the rutted track, spraying mud. Debris flutters from the branches of skeleton trees. The greyblack swathe of landfill stretches towards the city. On the far side, an old industrial district that went under in the flood. Buildings toppled on rotten foundations, the whole place built on sand, river sediment. We cut up past Rohan Island to a mile-long pedestrian tunnel under Žižka's horse, high on its hill, where the tomb of Stalin's puppet lies vacant & waiting.

The Enfield's reverb in the tunnel deafens. Yellow lights flicker overhead. And then we're in Žižkov, heading north again through fogged backstreets, grey worker's tenements walling them in. Tyres on cobblestones echo claustrophobic. Orange street lamps gloom like mortuary candles.

♠

We pull up in front of an ugly old white building that hunches up on itself – a 1920s cubist horror, wedged between office blocks, across the tramline from the cemetery. Blake unstraps a camera-bag from the back of the bike. It's part of what he does – photographing corpses. I listen to the ticking of the Enfield's engine as it cools. Across the road, people in black are milling around the cemetery entrance. A couple of kids are chasing one another between parked cars. As if on cue, an ice cream van drives by with a megaphone on its roof & a tinny polka drifting out of it. I settle down against a railing to watch the spectacle.

Blake comes over with his camera-bag slung across one shoulder, smoking a cigarette.

"Strange how families really only make a point of existing at weddings & funerals."

"It's why the commies tried to ban them most of the time," Blake yawns.

"Families?"

"Funerals. In public, death evokes primitive, tribal instincts. It always risks being political."

"And weddings?"

"Mindless optimism. Good for the masses."

"Is that why you brought me up here, to philosophise?"

Blake looks at me unsmilingly & shakes his head.

"There's something I want you to see."

He tosses his butt on the wet ground. Hiss. A dying insect on its back.

I follow him up a ramp to a loading-bay at the rear of the building. A couple of ambulances are parked off to one side. Blake speaks into a grill beside the bay doors & somebody buzzes us through. Inside it's mostly dark – a wide corridor with low-watt fluorescent tubes leads past rows of cubicle offices, pale hospital-green. A male nurse meets us at the far end of the corridor, he's wearing steel-rimmed glasses that stick out on either side of his head. One revolving fish-like eye. He looks like he might've been resurrected. *Dawn of the Dead.*

Blake mutters something to the stiff which gets lost in the general miasma. A wad of cash changes hands. The stiff gives me a fish-eyed stare & I stare back at him. Blake says something else & the stiff turns & jerks his head towards a set of double doors. We follow him through. Two orderlies in bleached overalls pass in the opposite direction. We approach another set of doors. No-one seems to speak. The silence is getting on my nerves. I want Blake to tell me what I'm doing here.

Next thing we're standing in the meat locker. Lights come on overhead. A row of sinks along a wall of scummed tiles that once were white. The stiff hands Blake a plain envelope then goes out. Without looking at it, Blake stuffs the envelope inside his coat. He's a pretty picture, with his fox fur, his silver hair flaring out, stubble & red eyes & flying goggles around his neck – like some Luftwaffe pilot blitzed on pervitin.

In the middle of the room a gurney has been left out, draped with a green sheet. Blake takes out his camera & walks over to it. He waits until I'm next to him before he pulls the sheet away. It takes a few seconds to register what

17

I'm seeing & then something inside me locks up. Bruised flesh leers pornographic – laughter, like a swarm of bees, swarming closer. I can hear the shutter of Blake's camera clicking off one shot after another until the film runs out. Somehow that sound neutralises everything.

♠

Behind my eyes images seethe & turn grey – my throat tightens around a scream that won't come out – my head goes numb. Regen's lying there, watching me. Red hair & jade eyes like an oriental fetish. A blur of stage-light on porcelain. Too naked. And then she's gone again. Where she lay, there's a corpse. Like a Janus figure. They might've been twins, but not quite. Two images reflecting one another through a gap in time.

Something happened once, ten years ago, in a place I want to forget. A memory, an image, a sickness. Old paranoias. I tell myself she's dead, but it sounds fake, as fake as when I tell myself she's alive, that she'll come back, that everything can still be the way it used to be. I close my eyes & open them again slowly, forcing myself to see only what's there. A slab of ruined meat. I can feel Blake watching me.

"It's not her," my voice flat.

I stare at the corpse's mouth while I repeat it – a black hole cropped out with teeth. "It's not her." Matted red hair. Eyes wide open, staring straight up – grey green, the corneas filmed over. Skin pale blue. But it isn't Regen.

There are bruises across the dead girl's breasts, her thighs. Crudely stitched autopsy incisions divide her abdomen. Crotch stubble. Abrasions on knees, shins, forearms. Supplicant. All of her fingernails are broken. Old rope burns wind around her wrists & neck like myrtle.

"How did you know?"

18

Without saying anything Blake pulls the sheet back over her. The gesture has an unnerving finality to it. I'm suddenly exhausted. The room seems much larger than it did before. There's a vaguely disgusting smell in the air. I feel Blake's hand on my arm & look up at him.

"Let's go," he says.

I look back at the crumpled green sheet – my hands, dead weights. I picture myself standing there like that. Inert. A thing.

Blake's walking away, towards the double doors.

I stuff my hands inside my coat pockets & follow him out into the corridor. The stiff in the lab coat's asleep on a chair. Somehow we retrace our steps through the labyrinth. Outside in the loading-bay the air burns my lungs. I'm sweating & cold at the same time, everything turning white, fog closing-in. I feel myself go down. The ground heaves, jerks upwards. Blake's voice is far away. I can't make out what he's saying. Dark whispers. Suddenly he's right in front of me, holding me by the lapels, backed against the wall. Something's wrong with my face. I reach my hands up. They come away wet. I don't know where we are. Then everything jolts back in time-delay.

"You hit me?"

"You passed out."

"I feel like hell."

"You look it."

"You said that before."

A grin pulls back from large yellowed teeth. He lights a cigarette, spits out a shred of tobacco. I wipe my face with a handkerchief. A clot of blood.

"Think you can stand on your own two feet?"

"It was the air."

"You'll get used to it."

# 3
## ORIENT EXPRESS

For every action there's supposed to be an equal & opposite reaction. Objects collide. Faces enlarge into proximity. Time burrows beneath the world leaving fault lines, tremors. Something inside us collapses, irrevocably. After so many years this is all there is. Night at our backs. The unwatched part of ourselves turns to nothing. It's for this we seek absolution. *Lord deliver us...*

Blake's head sways against the mist, the silhouettes of plain trees overarching the cemetery walls. A woman in a blue housecoat is raising the shutters in a stall selling red candles & funeral wreathes. She pays us no attention. The caretaker, in his fold-out chair, pares a cheese onto a piece of bread, a portable black radio at his feet – voices awash with static. I follow Blake under the metal archway, into the corner of the cemetery where the urns are kept in niches along the walls. Figures shift & huddle among the headstones, broken-off angels' wings, headless seraphim.

Neither of us speaks. I can't get the dead girl's face out of my mind. A glitch in time. Regen, ten years ago, standing on a bridge. A fake fur coat & blotted mascara that made her eyes into bruises under the streetlights.

An overturned bench sticks up from the foliage like a beetle with its legs in the air. Name after unrecognisable name, leached out of granite & sandstone. The feeling of something glimpsed over death's shoulder, shrivelled up, emotionless. Not knowing what keeps our obsessions alive. *Those eyes.*

We leave the cemetery by a side gate & head towards the freight yards. Back in the present Blake says something & I snap out of it. His voice like echoes under water, subliminal. Words back-masking their meanings. He's forcing me to think like this. Does he realise? Cracked & broken relics of things kept hidden. In times gone by, the secret art of the resurrection men. Death & sex. Naked corpses brought to life.

"A couple of days ago," he says, "they had a baby in there. Maybe a month old." Our shoulders touch. He doesn't flinch, gaze fixed inwards. "The mother was a junkie, gave the kid a shot to stop it from crying. You've never seen anything like it. Straight out of Zevio. They sent the mother up to Bohnice for electroshock. Figured she'd have to be crazy…"

I try to focus. Not *this*. Regen. The girl.

"Who is she?" I ask.

A long silence. Blake turns & looks at me, pondering.

"No-one knows," he says finally.

"Someone knows."

He shrugs, gazing straight ahead again, hands stuffed deep in coat pockets. The strip of road between the cemeteries seems colder, desolate. A tram wheezes past in the opposite direction, coming to a stop behind us.

"A couple of old guys snagged her with a fishing line down by Trója."

Brown water churning below the weir. Mist over the river. Silhouettes above the riverbank, of people watching. A body, hauled out, naked in grey light – delivered from the waters like something being born.

"When?"

"Yesterday."

"How'd you know?"

Blake glances back at me, the grey flesh around his eyes narrowing into slits.

"You're curious."

"Shouldn't I be?"

"Here," he says, reaching into his coat & pulling out an envelope. It's the same envelope he took from the stiff at the morgue. I give him a questioning look. "Something that might interest you." I take it & turn it over in my hands. "Read it inside," he says, nodding across the street. He tosses his butt on the ground, a dying note as it fizzes out.

♠

Behind corrugated iron sidings, freight yards cloaked in grey. Voices & engine noises float through the haze. We pass a barred gateway. A flatbed truck off-loading beer kegs. Dull clang as the large cylinders impact on concrete. To one side an old green dining car, jacked up on cinder blocks behind the buffers. A neon sign on top of it says: ORIENT EXPRESS. A faint glow filters through windows tinted nicotine brown. I follow Blake up the steps.

The moment we get inside the smoke takes my breath away. It tastes decades old. Low, covered lamps stand on each of the tables, casting the whole place in weird chiaroscuro. There's a couple by the door, old hatchet-faced types, in whispered conversation. A truck driver huddled in his coat, asleep, half-way down. We pick a table facing the yards & order brandy from a toothless blonde. When the drinks arrive we knock them back & order two more.

Inside the envelope are half-a-dozen typed pages. I spread them out on the table while Blake sits there staring at his glass. I can feel his intensity, waiting for my reaction. In front of me is a preliminary coroner's report. Bribed it off the stiff at the morgue. I wonder why he's doing this.

The report's a routine inventory. I scan through it then read back over the parts that catch my eye: Unidentified female Caucasian. 16-20 years old, 162cm tall, 64kg, red hair, green eyes. The dead girl bore identifying scars on both wrists & neck. She was deemed healthy. There was no alcohol in her blood stream at the time of death. Her lungs & stomach contained quantities of river water. There'd been haemorrhaging of the inner ear. Water pressure. Abrasions to hands, arms, legs. Post-mortem injuries. No visible lacerations to the vagina, rectum or perineum. Test for residues or foreign fluids inside the body: inconclusive. Circumstances of death: indeterminate. Cause of death: asphyxia from drowning.

Images flash. Rope marks on neck & wrists. Eyes wide open, staring. The river in grey winter daylight. Water churning beneath a weir. Barge or riverboat. A pair of fishermen dragging at something white in the water with a grappling hook.

"What do the cops say?"

Blake looks up from his drink.

"Treating it as suicide, is what I heard."

"How do they know she wasn't murdered?"

"Maybe they don't."

"What's that supposed to mean?"

"Impossible to tell, without evidence. Accident, murder, suicide – they all look the same."

"How many people do you know who drowned themselves?"

"Personally?"

"It's supposed to be…"

"Slow & agonizing." He looks away. "Though maybe, in the cold. Hypothermia. Who knows. It's not as uncommon as people think."

I try to picture it. It's night. Day. There's fog. No-one to see. She's standing there, on a bridge. Like Regen. Or else she's running, trying to escape? And then. She falls? Is pushed? Jumps? She begins by holding her breath, struggling against the current. It's freezing. Her body seizes up. A hand keeping her under? Turning her around? Disorientating her? Then something breaks. A spasm. She inhales. River water. What does it taste like? She vomits. An involuntary gasping for air. It goes on. Minutes pass. In the cold, it takes longer. Time slows down. Mind goes black, all reflex now. Nerves, muscle. Finally, it could take an hour for this, the brain suffocates. Dies.

I think: *Something made her choose this.* Then: *Did she choose this?*

I say: "She was naked when they found her?"

The muscle in Blake's jaw stands out. Prognathous. He prods another cigarette between his lips & lights it. Smoke eddies around the lampshade. Outside, the workmen have finished shifting the kegs. The sound of the truck's engine starting up.

"Does it matter?" Blake says. He looks straight at me. Showed me the dead girl for a reason. Didn't he? Wanly smiling. Do we ever know what's calculated? What isn't? A cockroach scuttles across the windowsill. I glance after it & it's gone.

"Suicides aren't usually naked, are they?"

"Aren't they?" A question answers a question. An echo.

I think: *In the middle of winter?*

He leans forward, the eye of his cigarette, thumb pressed to bottom lip. When he speaks, his mouth barely moves. He says, in a toneless voice:

"Would you like me to tell you a story?"

# 4

## SLIP KNOT

*Once upon a time*, my mother would begin, & then tell us the story of Hänsel & Gretel. Each time the story would be different, only the ending was the same. Like some complicated form of revenge being patiently worked out. All possible scenarios, all avenues of escape. I was little Hans, Regen was Greta. That was when we were children. We used to play together. Regen's family owned the vineyard behind our farm. In Autumn the grapes were harvested & made into wine. Burgundy, Saint Lawrence, Cabernet Franc. They used the old Sudeten word, *herbsten*. To harvest – to *autumn*. The dark grapes in the wine press. Yeast on the lees.

We'd always known each other, from before I can remember. Twins in a former life. Our families amazed us. Like characters in a story, they didn't seem real. We watched them act out their pantomimes of self-accusation, disappointed that the evil witch was never pushed into the oven, the wicked stepmother hacked to pieces, the impotent father given his comeuppance. Seasons dragged on. In summer we swam in the river & ate blueberries. There was an old bathtub set out among the vines, we never knew why. We'd lie in it at night & hunt constellations. I smoked my first cigarette there, got drunk on young wine. It was a lifeboat on a deadened sea, a womb or the bottom of a grave. It was easy to dream there.

Then everything changed. It happened on the eve of my eleventh birthday. On a Sunday morning, waiting for my mother to drive us to church. As usual I was dawdling behind the house, lobbing plum stones at the trees in the orchard.

There was something white hanging in one of the trees. It looked strange there. I went over to see what it was. Rotten plums burst underfoot. The ground was covered with them. Normally they'd have been collected in buckets, to make pudding, sauce, plum brandy. But normalcy went out the window that summer.

I remember the air around the trees thick with fruit fly. Bees swarmed from the hives at the foot of the orchard, a loud buzzing that came louder & louder the further I waded in. In the tree there was a bed sheet wound like a thick rope. A ladder rested against the trunk. On the ground beneath it was a pair of my mother's shoes, covered in ants. I stared at them, trying to connect them to the stockinged feet that hung down between the branches.

And then we moved away, into town, where my grandfather owned a butcher's. His father, too, had been a butcher. And his before him. Descended in a line unbroken from Cain.

After the move, I didn't see Regen again for a long time. I tried not to think about my mother, her stories had all been lies. Sometimes, after school, I'd watch my granddad re-sharpen his knives after butchering a pig, blood dripping from the skirt of his apron. Or I'd hide out in the cool room & set the carcasses swinging in the dark, finding poetry in the jangling of meat hooks & the cadences of jostled meat.

On weekends, when the weather was fine, I'd ride my bike out past the shoe factory & the abattoir on the edge of town, testing the forbidden distance back. The rich tang of the cesspools behind the abattoir with mist rising off them in winter. A tang like rotting plums. In school, when we studied Newton's law, it was the orchard I thought about. Things fall by force or gravity. The ripe plum-burst, the weight at the end of a damp bed sheet. Inertia. My mother had been a thin woman, dark-haired, constantly undergoing some form of malady. But she existed in the past like fiction.

Often I dreamt of my father, operating a machine with wheels & saw blades, & my mother like a pig's carcass being fed to it on a conveyor belt. For years I had the same dream. It always ended when my mother woke up, just before the machine was supposed to cut her in half. She'd open her eyes & instead of my father, she'd see me. And instead of her, I'd see Regen.

But now when I recall my childhood, what I think about most is the blankness. I try to picture myself as one of those happy faces in photographs, but it doesn't work. Happiness or pain, it's the same thing, only the pain seems more real. Some people think paradise is not being able to feel anything at all. Anaesthesia. You die that way. An organism can't exist without pain.

♠

Cue four years later. Regen at a bus stop, tall, in a light blue dress. I almost didn't recognise her. When she saw me, I don't know why, but I half expected her to hit me. For never having come back. But she didn't. We looked at each other without saying a word. There was something in her eyes time had intensified. Something fathomless & dark. I read the reflections there. Love & guilt. I was wrong. I didn't know how wrong I was.

The bus left us out in the middle of the vineyards. Dusk reddened the hillsides, the air full of insects. We crossed the fields towards Regen's house, down winding dirt paths, the trees along the river in silhouette. No-one was home. We took some wine & bread & lay out under the half-moon, in the old bathtub. We lay there naked. We whispered. We touched. The sky tilted on its axis.

I stared at my hands in the half-dark, combing the moonlight. Regen's hair, her back to my chest. She was humming a tune, like a nursery rhyme, quiet & repetitious. Lips & mouth.

Something irrevocable had come undone. It just happened that way. Without awareness. Without premeditation. The years of silence. Regen's pale body, her scent. The warm air.

"Once upon a time," she said, "a very poor woodcutter lived in a tiny cottage in the forest with his two children, Hänsel & Gretel."

Awkward laughter. Ghosts flitted between the vines.

"I'm sorry about your mother."

"You don't need to be."

"Did you ever think how in the story it's always the step-mother who's evil? Or the witch. And not the woodcutter. After all, they're *his* children. He tricks them into going into the woods. He knows what's going to happen to them. He knows it. But he pretends he doesn't. He pretends it isn't him who's killing them."

I felt drunk then, the air had turned cold. My hands looked too big in the moonlight. A flapping of wings.

"It's like they're his dirty secret," she said. "Little Greta & little Hans."

"Don't."

She turned & looked hard into my eyes.

"Don't what?" she said. And then her head jerked away. Like an animal, sensing intrusion. A shadow moved. Lights in the trees. Somewhere in the distance, approaching, washing over us. The crunch of tyres on gravel. A car door slammed. Footsteps. I sat up & followed Regen's gaze. A man was standing at the house gate, headlights casting strange shapes across the low stone walls. He seemed to be searching, stalking back & forth. And then he turned & stopped. I froze.

28

I felt his eyes burning holes in the dark. Neither of us breathed. He was looking straight at us.

♠

Before morning I hitchhiked back to town. It was further than I'd thought & almost no cars at that time of night. I walked through the pre-dawn until a flatbed delivering hay gave me a ride.

When I got home, he was waiting for me. I knew what was coming. He didn't even look up, just told me in a low calm voice to go to the laundry. It was cold in there. He took his time. I heard him come up behind me, unlooping his belt. He took me by the hair & pushed my head down into the sink we did the bleaching in. Fumes burned my nose & mouth. I screwed my eyes shut & prayed, a dumb inarticulate prayer full of fear, thinking how I should've run away, how I should've stayed with Regen. And then he whipped me like there was no tomorrow.

I lay on the laundry floor & shivered. It went on for hours. A crack of light under the stairway door told me my father was still awake upstairs. I imagined him up there, building & unbuilding some elaborate scheme of punishment in his mind. I began plotting my revenge, just as I always had, only now it almost seemed real. "Boy," he'd said. And he'd known. He'd seen right into me.

Afterwards, it took time for me to realise I could be stronger than he was. In my mind, I was still just an overgrown kid. On weekdays, before school, I lugged carcasses & meat trays for my grandfather. I fought off boredom by drawing pictures in my head. Every night I dreamt of Regen. I called from payphones. I rode out to meet her at the bus stop near the shoe factory. We walked to the wreckers yard. We made love on old vinyl car seats, pungent with diesel & engine grease. I started mulling over that first night. About how she hadn't been a virgin. About how I hadn't expected her to be.

My father said I was queer. He'd get drunk at his workbench, assembling & disassembling his machines, like an angry Archimedes. Machines for cutting, grinding, pressing. Killing & packaging machines. Antique machines that did nothing at all. I told Regen. About the drinking. About the anger. I said I thought it was because of mum. She said I could hit back if I wanted to. I told her about the fear. "Every fear," she said, "hides a wish." I thought about that for a long time. Psychology, she called it. The obvious turned backwards.

Regen's family were some weird religion that kept her out of school, but each Thursday she took the bus into town & borrowed books from the library. Her parents didn't care what she read. God spoke to them through their TV sets. She said apart from that they were open-minded. I asked what she meant, but she couldn't say. They belonged to a wine grower's cooperative. Every Autumn strangers came & harvested the grapes. My mother called them *Ketzern*, heretics. Said she pitied Regen. Her soul would burn, she said. Whenever Regen & I were together, she never took her eyes of us. Once she called Regen a little slut. It made me angry, though I wasn't sure why.

After we started seeing each other again, everything was different. It was as though I'd been asleep all those years. Regen knew things I'd never even heard of. When she talked to me, I came away feeling smaller, like I'd never be enough, never know enough, but aroused too, hungry to share the secret. I went to the library & borrowed the books she told me to. My father found them & laid into me. Said I was a lazy good-for-nothing cunt. Because I was old enough, he took me out of school & sent me to work at the abattoirs, to earn my keep. Each day four a.m. at the meat works. Knee-deep in blood & crap.

It pissed my granddad off that I wasn't around to do his donkey-work for him any more. They argued. My father said I should start earlier, work both ends. He knew I'd be too fagged-out to do anything about it. I got so tired I couldn't even dream anymore. On Thursdays Regen still waited for me. I memorised every inch of her & went over & over it in my head just to stay awake while we hacked up carcasses on a backwards production-line. My hands stank of dead meat. I conjured up the scent of her. My face between her thighs. The sun baking the car wrecks. The tang of our sex. Afterwards she'd read to me. About dreams, Nietzsche, poetry. Her words drifted over me like sleep. I felt more & more helpless. She asked me if I ever thought of killing anyone. I said *the smell of dead things clings to me*. She licked the blood from my fingers. She took me into her again & again. She made me forget these things.

# 5

## FETISH MACHINE

I want to know why Blake brought me to see the dead girl. I want to know where the rope marks came from. My mother hanged herself with a damp bed sheet, wound around a branch in an old plum tree. It would be easy to imagine it differently. A sheet spread on the ground, collecting the ripe fruit. A warm late spring morning. Lying there, gazing up through branches at the big sky. If I'd looked, would I have seen my mother's hands tied? The last act of someone who wasn't free. Childish thoughts come to me, of my mother climbing the ladder beneath that tree with both hands behind her back. Winding the sheet around the branch with her teeth. Slipping the knot. Falling. Only someone must've come & freed her wrists, because when they laid her out on the stretcher one arm stuck out from beneath the sheet they'd covered her with. A pale unblemished wrist. Fingernails bitten down to the quick.

Perhaps my mother hanged herself because she couldn't bear drowning. Perhaps the girl in the morgue drowned herself because she was at the end of a rope & life was strangling her. I don't know what drives a person to suicide. How many accomplices it takes. Who or what it is that decides. Empty causalities pile up like cairns erected to the dead. I see the drowned girl in my mind & I say to myself that I don't know her, I know nothing about her. But she stays there. She won't go away.

Blake knows about Regen. He knows I'm looking for her, only he doesn't know why. I ask *myself* why, & I don't know either. It's simply there, that's all, weighing like a fact.

Something that should've been self-evident, but wasn't. I need her to exist somewhere. To be possible. If I'd tried to understand it, the reasons would've gotten away from me. Just as she had. Just as she always had.

We're sitting there in the *Orient Express* like a couple of washed-up extras from a B-film no-one remembers ever having been made. Fumes of cooking fat & cheap liquor. A waitress with horrible girth hands us each a grease-smeared menu. We order brandy straight. The lampshade's shadow cuts Blake's face in half, one eye gone black. Dull aperture. Shutter blink.

"In ancient Rome," he says, Stoic-mouthed, "the punishment for murdering one's parents was to be scourged before being sewn into a leather sack – together with a monkey, a scorpion, a snake & a rabid dog. Then tossed into the river. The parricide's doom."

"It's customary," I say, "for God to smile upon the misfortunate."

I think: *You figure your odds. There's always a worse alternative to anything.*

Blake laughs. Crow-cackle. A disembodied head looming out of chiaroscuro. Eddies of cigarette smoke. Mouth open. Holofernes in Caravaggio.

"Do you know the story of Sotades the Obscene of Maronea?"

"Should I?"

"He was a poet from Alexandria. He invented the palindrome."

"The palin-what?"

"Writing something so it's the same backwards & forwards. Like D-E-D, dead."

"Sounds like a terminal disease." The marinated abscess pouring forth its poisoned parable.

"Terminal for some." Drone. "King Ptolemy had Sotades thrown into the sea wearing a lead suit, for scribbling satirical verses about his wife… Why he was called the obscene."

"Some people can't help themselves, I suppose."

Magor, I think. The mad poet, naked & drunk, pissing against the back-end of a Russian tank. Rotted in a cell in Valdice for the crime of poetry. Last seen: drowning his sorrows in a cellar under Jilská street, post-revolution. Magor who ranted: *Anyone can versify & go to hell for it. But that doesn't mean he's a poet.*

"Totalitarianism," Blake intones, "makes art into obscenity. Capitalism simply makes it idiotic. Like they used to say in the good old days: You kiss Marilyn Monroe's feet so you can be buggered by Stalin. Without his gaoler the artist withers & dies. Amen. He hates his freedom to be free. Amen. The monkey on his back. Amen. His father's corpse. Glory be to him who art. Amen. What should I be complaining about? We're free aren't we? Just look around. L'ironie c'est morte. Vive l'ironie!"

The waitress hovers, a toothless grin like a lopsided sphincter. Another brandy. Blake soliloquises. Somehow, without even moving his lips. The words emanate. Their shadows drift off through resinous air. The waitress returns again bearing a tray. I toss back the brandy. Scatter coins on the tablecloth. Silver & gold. Blake pokes yellowed fingers at them, slotting them back & forth as he speaks. The waitress snatches the lot, beating him at his own game. A loud guffaw.

"Vive l'ironie!" Blake stands & shouts.

"Do prdele!" belches the sleeping truck driver. *Up yours!*

Blake upends his drink. The fat waitress astride two bar stools.

"Baba Jaga," Blake says, with sly wink, twitch of mouth. "The furious child-eating witch."

A sour farting sound comes from her mouth.

*Goodnight sweet ladies...*

Blake exits stage left followed by yours truly. We stumble from the *Orient Express* & weave our way across freight yards. Labyrinths of drunken shipping containers stacked up into canyons. Rivers of slurried rainwater. Backwash. Ziggurats of scrapped steel. The drizzle once again peters out. A flare of grey light briefly in the east. At our backs. Unheeded epiphany. We stoop towards our shadows' blotted compass-point. Gravity. Footfall. Our echoes precede us.

Blake's monologue fractures, leads us through diversions, down blind alleys. He keeps hold of it barely, a blind man at the end of a leash. Blind leading the blind. Navigating through warehouses, shunting yards, past dilapidated sidings. We scale the junk mounds that border the old Jewish furnaces. *Židovské pece.* Lime kilns. Ghost smelters. Alchemists' covens. Up the brown weed-infested slope – our little mount of purgatory.

♠

Blake's studio is the attic of a building overlooking the yards. And beyond the yards, the faint outlines of poplars & yew trees in the cemetery where Kafka's ghost keeps company with the dung beetles. We ride the box elevator to the sixth floor. The grey concrete of the elevator shaft, scrawled with graffiti. Grey metal doors on each floor.

The studio opens off a small room with a couple of old office couches, a potted rubber plant & a pile of photo magazines. Blake throws his coat down on one of the couches & trails off through a doorway, camera bag slung low. He's still talking, reeling off names now of people who've taken the big swim in the Vltava. A type of telepathy, names dredged up from unconscious knowledge.

35

"Good King Wenzelsplatz," he says, mockingly, "had his ex-wife's confessor tossed off a bridge with his hands tied – the hapless John of Nepomuk. Otto Gutfreund, toady to Picasso, drowned himself there in 1927. The May uprising – '45 – corpses choking the river all the way to Dresden. So they say."

I follow the voice through a maze of tiny cubicles littered with film strips & contact sheets all reeking of acetone. A stairway up towards the high ceiling. A loft. Beneath it's the darkroom. Red light in doorway. "And of course," Blake says, leaning against a door jamb, "there was Pavel Tichý – 1995 – you probably never heard of him. A philosopher. Before the revolution, he wrote a thesis about the *vicious circle of definitions*. Suicidal algorithms of pure logic. But that was in another country. And besides..."

"History," he nods towards a curtained doorway, "is supposedly to blame." Turning his back. "Make yourself at home."

The door to the darkroom closes. I can hear Blake at work with his trays & chemicals – the alchemist's alembic distilling images from darkness into light. I wander around the studio, across the curtained threshold into the room he photographs his models in. A side wall with bookshelves & a workbench – a washbasin, a table littered with old prints, film cartridges, portfolios, empty whiskey bottles. Gel lights surround a plain square of herringbone parquet, painted black. A bolt of black fabric hangs down from black rafters. Black custom furniture with leather belts & metal rings attached.

In the silence of the room a faint sound of rain falling against heavily curtained windows. The room's cold & somehow empty, denuded. I flip through one of Blake's portfolios. The usual routine. Latex masks. Manacles. Fetish paraphernalia. I toss the portfolio aside & pick up another.

Faceless avatars bound in rope. Ankles, wrists, necks. Branded. Tattooed. Frame after frame of breasts, genitals, anuses. Mouths gagged, streaming spittle. Dead-eyed.

Blake calls this art, but he photographs corpses for money, though I don't suppose it's only for the money. Some studied higher purpose. Redemption of mankind. A line gets crossed somewhere. I mean, he's trying to photograph that line. The line between sex, death, the camera. The fetish inside the fetish machine. Camera-eye necrophilia.

♠

A camera, they say, has a perfectly clear conscience. Like God. Man staggers blind through a night of his own creating: his God exists to let him see with impunity the acts he's only able to commit by not believing in them. Like art. Or coincidence. Looking for clues to unravel some obscure crime. Only the mind creates disorder – everything that *happens* is a fact, born of an unknowable instant.

I'm standing there, Blake's catalogue in hand, filing through crime scene photographs, simulations, forensic nightmare banalities. A litany of detail, like a coroner's report. Each one offers up its scenario behind a veil of nakedness. On one page, a handcuffed penis, ridged with shadows of blue light. On the facing page, a blonde with artificially blue eyes, chained by the neck to a metal post. Two hands bound together supplicant. Eyes unfocused, a mouth disfigured by pain or boredom.

"Beautiful, isn't she?"

Blake's voice filling the malign silence. I hear the snap of a lighter. The burn of a cigarette.

"What's wrong?" His voice dry. "Got no stomach for it, have you?"

When I look up, Blake's standing there with a sneer that could cut ice. Coatless, he's cryogenically thin. He jabs his cigarette at something lying on the table. A sheet of photo paper slick with developing fluid. A face sheened with tears. Naked body. Autopsy stitches. Rope marks, lurid & colour-saturated. I feel my eyelids knot up into my head. There's an image in there, waiting for me. A face like the face in that picture. I can't describe what it belongs to. A demon with a hundred different bodies all sewn together into one.

"You're sick."

Blake snorts.

"The world's sick."

He takes down a fresh bottle from the bookshelf & breaks the seal. Whiskey. Pulls a squat vinyl armchair around to face me.

"Besides," he goes on, "what was it Rilke said? *Beauty's nothing but the beginning of terror*. But what can we know about beauty, without also seeking the meaning of terror? To lose yourself. To approach the nothing at the very heart of what we are. Terror is the great disillusionment."

It sounds pretentious & fake, like a justification. As fake as the pain in his photographs. I say nothing. Lay the portfolio down on the workbench & reach out for the print he's left lying there. My hands shake. I try not to look at them: *It's just the body of a girl someone found in the river*. The developing fluid has dried into blemishes like a film of scum on brackish water. I try to work the tension out of my jaw. There's more to all this, but I'm not sure what. Everything's too obvious, obscure. Finally the words come.

"You knew her?"

He looks at me blankly.

"If you say so," he says.

38

He takes a long swig from the bottle. Wipes his mouth with the back of his hand. His eyes are almost black with dilation, red around the rims. He's been doing lines in the darkroom between stages. Bugging-out on pervitin. He offers me the bottle. I shake my head. I look again at the photograph.

"She's all yours," he says. "Keep her. A souvenir."

I fold the picture & stuff it in my coat pocket.

"You know," Blake says, "people must wonder about you." He takes another swig of whiskey. "The way you hide out on that bucket of rust, cutting up fucking magazines. All that voodoo crap. Looking for a girl who maybe doesn't exist. Talking about it the way someone talks about a crime they maybe committed in their sleep."

I walk around behind him, barely listening. There are dead flies at the foot of the curtains, mingled with dust & hair. I pull one of the curtains back & look out at the rain. The weather won't make it's mind up. It'll go on like this all day. Like an accusation. I turn & stare at the back of Blake's head. A mess of silver hair sticking up above the headrest.

I say: "Something's on your mind. You've been stringing me along all morning."

I think: *I'm to blame?*

Because I can't help remembering that time with Regen in the wrecker's yard & how she kept on asking me, while I'm fucking her, coming inside her, if I'd ever wanted to kill someone. Fingernails stabbing into the base of my cock, sweat gleaming on her neck, on her sternum. Only now when I see her, there at the back of my mind, she's holding a camera in her free hand pointed straight at me. I picture a line-up, mug-shots, police reports. I see myself becoming part of the evidence for a crime that hasn't taken place yet.

Blake laughs dryly. Another swig. Another movement of the hand across the mouth. I suddenly feel too tired to give a damn what he thinks. The sort of hell he lives in. Demons talking.

"I think sometimes there are just too many coincidences." Fingers pinching the bridge of his nose.

"I don't believe in coincidences," I say.

"No," he says. "Of course you don't."

# 6
## ULTRAVIOLET

Sometimes I wonder if Blake really exists, or if I really exist, or if we made each other up as alibis. A chance encounter on the other side of the world. You open your mouth to speak & they recognise you. The foreigner. The toy of paradox, forever out of place: a man running through a desert watched by a silent audience, struggling towards the invisible reprieve. A desert full of mirrors.

La Paz, in the last days of December. The old year gasping its last. Treading the path of dissipation, amnesia, absolution. A journey with a wrong symmetry, across an ocean & two continents. A journey that began when Regen disappeared. Losing track of the cause. Tunnelling down into my nightmare, to the child no-one has found or ever will find. A child in an orchard staring at a plum tree. The child I long to lay to sleep at night. To dream again, to never have to wake.

After all these years.

But at the end of the nightmare, I find Blake. Slouching by a newspaper stand, under the eaves of a bus station in La Paz. Rain slanting down through polluted air. Waiting for me. The way a complete stranger waits for you, to take possession of your life. A djinni. A spirit. The shadow of a rope dancer weaving your soul into bondage.

♠

Six years later. Paris. A ship back across the Atlantic. A train from Le Havre. Escape had been useless. I knew where it had

41

to end, even then, staring through the train window at row after row of chimneys rising above an unfamiliar horizon, black smoke billowing into the sky. An orange sun hovered there, like a fragment of a dream fading. Wheels shunting on tracks.

The sound of the wheels goes far back. All the way to the Amazon, staring at the sun rising over the vast river delta – the black sun reborn. Believing I too had been reborn. The old flesh worn away, scarified, purified. The past, cast off like fiction. Who would know me? I held onto the image of Regen, unfallen, untainted by what I'd forced myself to know. To become. Like the prodigal son on the eve of return, his crimes cast behind him like a shadow grown thin with the approach of midday.

But at the Gare St Lazare I waited on a bench, not knowing what to do. Like a prisoner stepping back out into the world. With each day crossing the ocean, my paranoias had increased. I sank down into my captivity. Born of the great river, now once again nothing but a man inside a body inside a room. The inner room & the outer room. The room of the mind & the room of the universe.

There's never any way out. Held hostage by a past you're unable to confront & a present that escapes you. You stare at a crack in a wall, never thinking what you'd do if you ever found yourself all of a sudden on the other side. Or the other side doesn't exist. You step through & immediately you're where you started again. Like a crime you're destined to commit & go on committing, time without end. A crime made pointless. Because the victim's already dead.

The ghosts multiply. The places you return to are more than meets the eye. I imagined myself going backwards through time, to that moment on the bridge, in the rain, with Regen's face dissolving & reforming. There. Forever *there*.

And all I'd have to do is reach out my hand & touch her. The light in her hair, falling across her bare shoulders. Caressing her. The way I longed to caress her.

But I wasn't there yet. Sitting on a bench, in the Gare St Lazare. Unfamiliar faces on every side enlarging into proximity. After a while I noticed a black woman sitting opposite me, her head in her hands, sobbing. How long had she been like that? I didn't know. I looked around, but the crowd moved as though it'd fallen asleep. It was a sleep I longed to join. To become nothing but a particle in a human tide. To see & hear nothing. But still I waited. The woman seemed to go on crying for hours. I tried to say something to her in French. I lent over & touched her shoulder. Her hair. Her face. She looked up in confusion. I imagined her recognising me, like a lost child come home. Smiling through her tears. Embracing me. Covering me with her mouth. Taking me home to some shithole in the *banlieue*.

I saw my reflection in the woman's eyes. It made me feel sick. I wanted to wrench it out. A deep fear came into me & I ran. A man in a dirty suit, with an old duffel bag, rushing headlong into the crowd like a thief. Inhuman voices pursued me onto the street. I staggered blindly. Everything blurred. My mind travelled alone through its darkness. Eventually I wandered into the Marais. Off rue de Rivoli I walked into a bar. And there was Blake, sitting at a table, counting his cigarettes. He was thin & pale, his eyes seemed to have sunk into his skull, & his hair had turned grey.

But he was expecting me.

♠

In Bolivia we'd both had different names. Different names, different histories. He wasn't a photographer yet then. During the last of the uneventful years, the *nomenklatura* had him shovelling shit at a pig farm in Lety for his sins. After the revolution, he took the first plane out, fucking his way around the world. Bogotá. La Paz. Rio de Janeiro.

When I sat down he didn't even look at me, just told me to buy the next round. I said I didn't have any money & he laughed, a dry sardonic laugh.

"Don't worry about it. Neither do I."

An old Algerian barman out of a film by Clouzot set down a carafe of *vin blanc* on the table, beside an empty one already there.

"*Na zdraví!*" Blake said. "Here's to old etceteras."

We drank & watched the traffic. The barman brought another carafe. It got dark. We drank some more. Another carafe. The barman. Replay after replay in slow motion. The traffic like a tin orchestra, rattling out an accompaniment to the old man's underwater dance. Flies circled above the table at half-speed. It couldn't go on, I thought. I told Blake I was going back. Prague. He nodded profoundly.

"Kafka called Prague a malignant old sow."

"Kafka was an insurance salesman."

"Naturally," he said. "It pays to expect the worst."

I wondered vaguely about what would happen next. Blake pointed across the street at a bike parked on the sidewalk. A black Enfield Bullet.

"What do you think of that beauty?" he said. "A wise old Indian left it with me as collateral. Would you believe they still make them in a factory in Bombay? Just like the originals." He stood up. "Let's get the hell out of here."

♠

Fast forward. It's too late or too early. September becoming October. The between-seasons. Along the Boulevard St Michel, advertisements in light-boxes illuminate pools of vomit on the sidewalk, bums asleep behind umbrellas & cardboard boxes in doorways. As I walk it begins to feel as if something's spilling out of me, trailing on the street, unravelling like intestines. The gutters are full of me. With each step more of me is oozing out. I turn around & expect to see the rats at work, gnawing at my entrails. But there's nothing. Tarmac & dead neon. Ultraviolet.

Four a.m. on the Pont Neuf, I begin throwing up. It doesn't stop until there's nothing left inside. I vomit so hard my eyes bleed.

An hour ago I was laughing my head off on Denfert Rochereau. *Rock'n'roll Hell*. Blake & the Spaniard were dancing under a streetlight. I left them there, fixed in my mind like two figures in a postcard. Before that, a narrow brick house on the Passage Barrault & Blake's half-room apartment. A red light over the toilet & contact sheets hanging everywhere. He'd started photographing the girls he picked up on the street with an old Flexaret. Crude black & white. Stripped. Needle-eyed. He's begun to make a name for himself. He's going back to Prague, too, to have an exhibition in some gallery that's supposed to be famous.

The ride across Paris had been a blur. The Marais. The Seine. The lights of the Boulevard St Germain. Alphaville. Nameless streets winding into the night.

We sat on a balcony drinking Japanese beer & rum, watching the dull halo of the city. Darkened façades like expired film stock. He talked about the women he'd known. About revolution & death squads. Argentina. El Salvador. Mexico. Cuba.

"History's all about copping it sweet & thinking you've got it made."

"Yeah. And they say we had a velvet revolution." Sure. Velvet like a whore's skirt worn thin at the back. Or not even velvet, but some cheap imitation, *velveteen*.

"Fuck the revolution," Blake said.

He brought out a film canister full of white powder & began cutting up lines. We got high. It was La Paz all over again. A grimy courtyard room with flies asleep everywhere. Stained mattress on the floor where a waterfall cascaded through the ceiling whenever it rained. I'm sitting on a chair, hypnotised by the sound of mosquitoes, water dripping. I hear Blake on the phone. He's calling someone. He says it's a whore he knows. Spaniard. We do more lines. Blake passes a joint. It's heavy stuff. Silhouettes flap their wings – a flock of crows. Echoes multiply. Distant orchestras tune their strings.

Later there are voices. A man's & a woman's. I can hear somebody breathing, too hard. My chest thuds. There's a muffled cry. I wake up. Blake's standing at the balcony railing with a woman bent-over in front of him, her skirt hiked up above her waist. I guess it's the Spanish whore he keeps talking about. There's a pillowcase over her head, tied at the neck. He's running his fingers in & out of her arse. Legs spread. Her hands reaching back, cuffed. Light glints on her fingernails. The sound of her breathing.

Blake turns to me, a humorous look in his eye.

"Fuck her," he says.

His camera's on the table. A Flexaret, antique. The lamplight from the apartment falls across their bodies at wrong angles, like montage. I struggle to my feet. My head swims. The back of my neck's wet through the collar of my shirt. I try to focus on the sliver of light across the girl's left thigh. It snakes in & out. Blake's grinning at me. He says:

"Just like old times."

She stands there, immobile, a mannequin. Something conjured out of nowhere. Le Paz. Paris. I look down & see my cock half-stiff in my hand. A thing. An instrument. I hear the Spanish whore laugh. I reach out with my free hand & grip the pillowcase around her neck, her torso across the railing. And then I'm fucking her. Or somehow she's fucking me. Stuffing me in her. The shutter of the Flexaret rasping. The night sky wheeling.

# 7
## FIESTA PIG

Kafkaville. It's after midday when I leave Blake passed out in his studio with a half-empty whiskey bottle. The pavements are cracked & subsided, banked with mud & melted snow. Grey, brown, black. There's only a slight mist of rain now. Umbrellas. I pass an all-night cinema showing old Mario Bava films. *La Frusta e il corpo.* A poster with Christopher Lee brandishing a whip, the tail of it coiled around Daliah Lavi's wrist. Low budget phantasmagorias. At the intersection, people waiting like people always do. Fog seeps up from the river valley.

I find a seat on the next tram that comes along & sit there looking at my hands. Ex-slaughterer's apprentice. It's hot inside but I'm shivering. Outside the fog turns everything into contradiction as we descend towards the river, making immediate what's impossibly remote, the proximate turned unfathomable. The world slides away as sleep takes hold of me, summoned to dreams of future refinements of killing. I see my father working his machines. Gutters of blood & offal. The huge fiesta pig stuffed with little pig corpses.

The tram's downtown already when someone jostles me & I wake up. Václavák. Wenceslas Square. I stagger out into the weather, crowds on the sidewalks, cling to walls under eaves, press against the flow, collar pulled up, water in my eyes. I escape the Square into a maze of narrow cobbled streets – a cluster of bars & non-stops, & then the boarded-up courtyard where the brothels used to be. Behind it, the old Temple district, & a bar called the *Marquis de Sade.*

It doesn't even begin to live up to its name. The entrance is plain with a few tables & chairs spilling onto the pavement & a sign painted in red & black. A naked lightbulb hangs over the doorway. I push through a pair of swinging saloon doors as a peroxide blond in a black miniskirt comes staggering out. She trips, smashing her face into the wall. The smell of alcohol & sex trails behind as she recoils onto the street. Inside, the usual circus is going on. The dregs Saturday night left behind.

I shake the rain from my coat & head for the bar. When I sit down I get the feeling the barman doesn't like the cut of me, so I give him my ugliest smile & order brandy for two. There's a girl sitting alone a couple of stools away. Under the dull glow of the lights, she looks like just another hustler on the downslide, except she's reading a book at the bar the way Regen used to. I slide the second drink over & she looks up, glass-eyed. Could be worse. Short & blond with a starved face. A black, high-necked sweater, black skirt & boots.

"Not interested," she says, looking at the drink. Then she takes a closer squint at me. "I don't know you." It's a statement, not a question.

"Sure you do," I tell her. "We've known each other for centuries."

"Whatever," turning her attention back to the book.

"What's the main attraction?"

She shakes her head, dismissive. Then looks up with eyebrows comically raised, all mock gravitas now:

"Aristotle."

I can't help laughing.

"Here's to old man Aristotle, then." I tip back the brandy & signal the barman for a refill. He nods at the girl. I see she's emptied hers, too. Cute. I jerk two fingers at the barman. Sure, drinks are on me kid. He even manages a grin.

Seen this before. Well so what? I didn't come here for anything. I wait for the barman to make himself scarce then take another look at the girl. She's watching me, eyes not glassy anymore.

And then it's ten years ago. The end of the night, in a border town strip club. The *Ace of Spades*. A cellar done up like a medieval dungeon. The place stinks of booze, cigarette smoke & sweat. You can imagine people having died there in despair, broken, souls dislocated from bodies & dunged-out with the rest of the effluent. I look around, getting my bearings. The place is almost empty except for the fixtures in the front row, too drunk to move. A dancer who's seen better days is going through the motions & already down to her last trick when I make the bar. By the time I've crossed to the back of the room the stage is empty. It hardly makes a difference. My eyes aren't on the stage anyway. I'm looking at Regen.

She's sitting alone at a back table, reading a book. A black fake fur coat & fake leather boots. I know when I see her that I'm afraid of what'll happen next. She's changed already in the weeks since she ran away. She's dyed her hair. Blonde. It catches the red neon. Her fingers tap the side of a glass as she reads. Long, jade-green fingernails. I search her face, blotted mascara making her eyes into bruises. It's a while before I realise she's staring back at me. A black basilisk stare. It's obvious she knows I've been looking for her. All along the border, one sleaze pit after another. Trying to pick up her trail. Almost losing her.

The moment's an anticlimax. I don't know how I imagined it should've been. Seeing myself now, standing there in that bar, staring at the blonde in the black coat. I feel the bouncer behind me waiting for a sign. Regen shakes her head. Slowly. Telling him we're old friends. I don't even know what that means, but my legs are going weak. I sit down. We seem so remote, then, facing one another across that table. I think of visiting-hour scenes in old prison films. The man doing time for his woman, who brings him cigarettes once a fortnight & tells him she's saving herself for the day he gets out.

After a while I realise she's smiling at me. My face twists into something ugly, but I guess I'm smiling back at her. We're both smiling together.

♠

Back in real time, in the *Marquis de Sade*, it's pushing mid-afternoon. They've replaced the earlier crowd with an even seedier one. The music's decades old & getting older. The next three tracks are all *Walk the Line*. It's a grind. I figure listening to Johnny Cash is like having the piles. Then it switches to something more upbeat. Tom Waits. *God's away on bizniz*. And ain't that the truth. Some blow-hard hangs on my elbow & starts giving me the spiel about how music sold out. I tell him to breeze. The barman smears a dirty rag over the zinc-top.

When I ask, the girl at the bar says her name's Inessa. From a mill town, where the Ucha meets the Serebryanska, some shithole called Pushkino. It conjures all sorts of things: Soviet cinema gulags for dead poets. She looks older than she probably is. Says she's a student at the university. Doesn't talk much. I prefer it that way anyhow. We finish the best part of a bottle of brandy in near silence. Later when we're fucking she's as quiet as a corpse. In the boarded-up passageway opposite St Jakub's church, her face against the wall, eyes screwed closed. I make believe it's Regen. In my head I'm fucking her & she's laughing so hard I have to hit her to make her stop.

51

But it's only in my head. I tell myself to get a grip. Inessa just stands there wiping between her legs with a dirty handkerchief, eyes glistening in the dark of the passageway, too young & too old. I reach out & she cowers, half-expecting the blow that doesn't come. Something wrenches at me & I feel my fist smash into the wall. Those eyes, that dumb animal look, like an accusation. I reel out into the rain & let it soak into me. I want to scream. The sky falling down. The raw air. And there's Inessa, in front of me, punching me in the chest with both hands as hard as she can, cursing in bitch Russian, so furious it makes me laugh. A mad laugh, mouth open to the rain & her, in her sideways heels, flailing for all she's worth. Until the laughter gets into her too. And then we're both laughing, like a pair of idiots out there in the rain, in the empty street.

We kiss then, the way children do. Blindly. Selfishly. Something like tenderness comes over me. She's shivering. This frail, unknown thing. I take her in my arms & carry her across the street out of the rain into the church. Beneath the archway, through the wooden doors, along the aisle. The smell of scented tallow hangs in the air. I lay her down on a pew & rest beside her. Her head on my thigh, my coat draping her. In the silence of the church she drifts into a fitful sleep. I sit & watch the light falling through the stained glass windows. The martyrdom of the saints. The miraculous birth. Death & resurrection. Light falling through darkness. Darkness into light. The eternal contraries.

A watery voice calls through an alcoholic haze. Some kind of music. I open my eyes & Inessa's standing there watching me, comical in my oversized Gestapo coat. I can't help laughing.

"Vole!" she says. *Ox.*

People turn & notice us. They're filing in for the afternoon service. A herd of swaying bovine faces, avid for penitence. *And the fool has said in his heart "there is no God."* I grin back foolish. Let them take their God to hell with them. Hanged son of man in the laughing tree. My pious mother stands there, evangelising the false sinners in purgatory. *Ave Maria, gratia plena, dominus tecum. Virgo serena, pia, munda et immaculata.* Dismayed whispers follow us onto the street. Inessa, her matted hair, mascara bleeding down her cheeks. An angel driven from door to door. I kiss her face, brush her wet hair back with blunt fingers, standing over her in my undertaker's suit. What dreamless charity settling the old accounts?

Arm in arm we wind the narrow backstreets to Pařížská, past the la-di-dah restaurants, the hotels & boutiques. We run pell-mell along the crowded sidewalks, leaving chaos in our wake. Over the river, towards the broken metronome on the hill where Stalin's colossus used to be. A monument to how little times change.

Halfway across the bridge, we stop to gaze at the seagulls brooding on the water. At the blue & white boats moored along the quays. The bronze, peasant-thighed angels atop their pillars, gazing blankly down at us. A tram thuds by in the direction we've come, steam rising from the tracks in its wake. We move on, climbing the steep stairway to the dead metronome, with its red needle lying on its side. Built to fail. The mist has risen under grey-black clouds. Denuded suburbs lie with haunches spread. A faint drizzle makes everything faintly glisten.

# 8
## ACE OF SPADES

Old man Aristotle once said that children are incapable of noble acts & so can't be truly happy. The first time Regen ran away she was fifteen & pregnant. I didn't know it then. She simply disappeared. One Thursday in April she wasn't waiting at the bus stop & so I went looking for her. At the farmhouse I found her parents in front of their idiot box, listening to God. I waited. Her room was full of unreturned library books. Clothes in the cupboard. An old porcelain doll on the bed. I couldn't connect the room with Regen at all, except for the books. I realised I didn't know anything about her, only her body & what she talked about while I lay beside her dreaming.

On the way back to town I questioned the bus driver. He knew her, said maybe she'd got off at the train station in Božice that morning. That's when I knew. It was a small station on the edge of the woods, there was only one directions to go. I hitched the six o'clock train west without thinking twice. I had my week's pay from the meatworks in my pocket. My old man could go hang himself.

After the capitalist revolution, the border became a Mecca for cheap sex, with Znojmo at the centre of it. I guessed straightaway why Regen might've gone there. If you wanted to disappear, it was as good a place as any. Without money & underage, there weren't too many options anyway.

That first night I walked all over Znojmo looking for her in vain. I put out the word the way only dumb kids in movies do. A bum at the train station said he'd seen her in the guise of a virgin with angels' wings & for fifty crowns would show me where. Taxi drivers snickered. Barmen swore they'd spotted her with a negro, a Russian gangster, a German with a moustache. A real comedy act.

I got wise & copped to the routine, the faces on the street, the pick-up zones, the places to find the low-down on fresh meat. The first day, I slept under a bridge & woke up smelling like a drain. After that, I stayed in stairwells & doorways until one morning a couple of skinheads kicked me awake & one of them pissed on me. I grabbed the one with his cock sticking out & hit him in the face. I didn't punch him hard but I felt bone crunch. Teeth sprayed on the pavement. The cunt just stared down at them & cried, face all jelly. His boyfriend sprinted, screaming his head off. I expected dozens of skinheads to come barrelling in any second. But none did. I ran anyway. When I got to the corner I looked back & saw the skin who'd pissed on me kneeling on the pavement, picking his teeth out of a pool of blood. I almost felt sorry for him. But didn't.

I'd been doing it rough for a week & was just about skint, & my bright idea of finding Regen wasn't getting me anywhere but down. I didn't know what else to do, though I'd already decided I wasn't going back, not for anything. While I was figuring out my next step, a waitress I'd got friendly with suggested I ask up at the brewery for work. I didn't have any better ideas. The Hostan Brewery was on a hill above the town. I went & waited there for the foreman to show until mid-afternoon, standing in the courtyard like an idiot in the spring rain, getting a free wash.

The first thing the foreman told me was to bugger off. But I just grinned my dumbest grin & stayed put. It must have got the better of him because the next thing I knew I was riding in the back of a truck delivering kegs. I went there again the next day & did the same thing, dawn till dusk, with plenty of thinking time in-between. We drove everywhere. After a week, I reckoned I knew every table dancing joint, every cabaret, strip show & claphouse on the border. And it was only then that I heard about the *Ace of Spades*.

♠

It was a nurse at the abortion clinic who'd offered to help Regen find a job & a place to stay. Quid pro quo. No questions asked. The job was at *The Ace*, a strip club off the main drag heading south out of town. It was a white two-storey joint with blacked-out windows & a big red neon playing card stuck over the door. The first couple of nights I went there, Regen didn't show. Each night I waited through half-a-dozen routines, shelling out for drinks I didn't want. I stayed until morning. The third time around I slipped the stooge at the bar a large note & asked about a redhead with green eyes. He looked me over & shook his head. "Redheads are trouble, kid." He pocketed the note I'd given him anyway. Said maybe to come back the day after. I was nearly out the door when he called over. "It's not a redhead you're looking for, kid. It's a blonde."

I couldn't sleep & the next day I worked both shifts. I was on edge, adrenaline keeping me awake. If I didn't find her now, I was lost. All I could think about was Regen, her face, her body under my hands. And her mouth. Her lips against my ear, whispering into me.

It was long after midnight when I made it back to the *Ace*, hitching from the town square. The barman was right – her hair was blonde now, straight out of an old Lana Turner film. Sitting alone at the back of the room, reading a book. She put the book away before I could see what it was. Staring up at me with depthless eyes. I didn't know what to say, so I said nothing. We had a couple of expensive drinks & she did the talking for both of us. Told me she'd been doing tables, learning the ropes. She'd ended her shift. She didn't seem surprised to see me.

After some more drinks that tasted of nothing, Regen suggested we go upstairs. I paid the man at the door, like anyone else. The room was dark & small. The windows blacked-out. It looked wrong, like it didn't belong anywhere. A room outside the world.

In the dull glow of a table lamp, I watched as she lay back across the bed & stretched out her legs so that her skirt slipped up to the top of her stockings, jaw tense with desire. I wondered how the ritual unfolded normally. She read my thoughts.

"I'm not a whore," she said, matter of fact.

I stood over her, with a dumb ugly look on my face, wanting her. She pulled me down, her boots over my shoulders, wet nylon parting her sex. Scent of patchouli. I pulled the strip of nylon aside. She moaned as I tongued her. My thumb worked into her arse as my hand cradled her. Boots cold against the back of my neck. Tongue tipping her clitoris the way it tipped the letter *t* in *Baťa*.

I fell asleep inside her. It was a sleep like I'd never experienced before. Ten years passed in ten minutes. A river floating under the world. An endless passageway filled with vines, strange roots, undead things. I saw Regen in the dim light & held out my arms to clasp her, but she slipped back into the darkness. And then she was shaking me awake. A suitcase by the bed. Downstairs she took me straight past the bouncer at the door. I'd expected some type of stand-off. It didn't happen.

We stood out in the car park, looking at the road. Intermittent traffic flowed by, heading south on the E59. The Austrian border was only a minute away. Thousands of

Sudeten Germans had been marched there at the end of the war. *Der Brünner Todesmarsch*. Beaten & raped by Pokorný's revolutionary guards. Regen's grandmother, I knew, had been among them. Some sort of atavism seemed at work. The unconscious return to the scene of a barely remembered crime. Justice or amnesia. *And what good's a crime that goes unremembered?*

I realised, standing in the car park of the *Ace of Spades*, that the myth of our childhood was ending. We began to walk in silence along the motorway north, away from the border zone. A pair of unlikely fugitives. Regen with her boots & her black coat trailing behind, me with her suitcase. Her bleached blonde hair caught the headlights like a halo. It reminded me of a picture I'd seen once. Over-exposed.

We walked all the way into town. Never once did anyone slow down to give us a ride. At the train station we waited. A bench on the platform, our bodies folded into each other beneath that fake fur coat of hers. The smell of her perfume & the smell of effluent on the tracks. As dawn broke, the sky above was green with thunder clouds. They hung there like horrible grapes about to burst.

# 9
## ST PAULI

There's a picture I used to carry around with me, a print from an old disposable camera. It showed Regen, standing behind my father, framing his face with her hands. Like a trophy. I found it among the things she left behind. In the background there was a wall with magazine cut-outs. A room in the last place we were together – a place someone named the Snake House. It was an old cottage on a farm near Božice, right by a lake near where we grew up. I found the photograph in the same room it was taken in. He was sitting on the edge of the bed & she was kneeling behind him. She'd put the camera on the dressing table & set the timer. But the flash hadn't gone off. The picture was underexposed, the faces slightly blurred. You could still make out the remote look in his eyes. And the faintly mocking look in hers.

On the train from Znojmo, Regen told me everything. In one way or another. About the abortion. About how my father had forced himself on her. From when she was thirteen. How her parents had ignored it. How she'd wanted to kill herself. How she'd always been too afraid to tell me. Afraid I'd blame her for it, too. The look in her eyes when she said it. Everything else dissolved into blackness. The train compartment, the scenery through the compartment window, the voices outside in the passageway. If I close my eyes now, it might all cease to have existed. The world falls away. There were only words, none of them real.

In my mind's eye I saw her strapped into a machine & him mounting her like a pig, his snout grovelling in her sex, violently rooting out her innocence. I recalled my mother's words – how she used to call Regen a slut. And now I understood, it hadn't been on my account. All that crap about Hänsel & Gretel! She'd known the truth. And that terrible knowledge had driven her to suicide?

Everything came together in a single, horrible revelation. I knew then that it'd been him that first night at Regen's house, standing in the headlights. I was sure of it. He'd warned me never to go back there after my mother's death, after we'd moved away. But it hadn't been me he'd come for that night. It was her, Regen, knowing her parents would be away. He'd raped her, she said, right there in the house, in the bedroom I'd never seen until the day she ran. But in that photograph, of the two of them together, at the very end, I couldn't see any of that. The fear, the hate. Only a man & a girl, who could almost have been his daughter. It gave me a funny feeling.

I swore on the train to Prague that I'd kill him. That I'd butcher him a thousand times over. Obliterate every particle of him so that nothing at all would remain. I let my fury sweep over me. And still that look in Regen's eyes. I couldn't tell what she saw, but I felt she *pitied* me. I wondered how she'd looked at him & if she recognised him in me. My very blood was poison. The stranger who'd coupled with my mother to make me. What idea could he have had of my existence? He who created & despised me. His own flesh & blood. Did he know me before he made me? Did he think of me as he was making me? The way he thought of his machines. Obsessing over them, caressing them with his mind, in that secret part of himself that might even have been human.

But my anger overwhelmed me & made me weak. Like a boy in a fairytale who pretends to take destiny by the horns & finds himself gored by his own fear. I thought of the child

Regen had killed. My brother or sister inside her. My helpless double. My doppelganger. I didn't know what to feel. My first thought was that the child should've been mine. It was only later that I asked myself how she could've been so sure – who the father was.

♠

The train journey seemed as though it'd never end. Žerůtky, Moravské Budějovice, Lukov, Bohušice, Popovice, Lesůňky, Horní Újezd, Kojetice, Čechočovice, Hvězdoňovice, Okříšky, Přibyslavice, Číchov, Bransouze, Dolní Smrčné, Přímělkov, Bítovčice, Přeboř, Petrovice, Bradlo, Malý Beranov, Hruškové Dvory, Jihlava. Then north, to Havlíčkův Brod, Sázava, Čerčany. The place names multiplied. They flashed past like time itself made visible in a blur of syllables. I began to lose track of where we were & where we were going.

All of a sudden we were in the eastern suburbs of Kafkaville. Říčany. Kolovraty. Strašnice. Malešice. The factories of Karlín. The monument to one-eyed Žižka. And then the grey dingy ironwork of the Woodrow Wilson train station – Hlavní Nádraží – aswarm with hawkers, hustlers, money-changers, pushers, pimps, pickpockets & panhandlers. Gateway to the Golden City.

I waited in front of the station on a park bench while Regen went to find a place to stay. She said she had an aunt. She made some phone calls. I sat on the bench with Regen's suitcase & watched the junkies shooting up behind the hedges. There was a blue sky. It hurt my eyes. I must have been crying. An impotent, exhausted rage. It was dark by the time Regen came back. The streetlights had come on. I heard her calling my name across the park. I'd almost forgotten what I was doing there. In the lamplight she was like an apparition. A fallen angel. She kissed me.

61

Her aunt lived on the south side of the river, in a shared apartment overlooking the docks. There was a bar downstairs, a small-time claphouse called *St Pauli*. Like the district in Hamburg. I didn't think about it at the time – maybe it was a coincidence. I suppose you could say everything that happens is some sort of coincidence – only some things are more coincidental than others. You get to thinking there's a demon in the works, stacking the odds. Keeping everything on the downslide.

The tiny room we stayed in had a crucifix on the wall & a green couch stuffed with horse hair for a bed. There was a window above the couch, grimed with coal dust, facing the river. I'd watch the freight being unloaded on the docks in the afternoon & then head-out at night to work shifts wherever I could find them. Most times I hung around the bars killing time until morning, when it was clear to go back. Our room – the room we thought of quaintly as ours – was for rent nightly by the hour. Regen worked tables, paid our board. She kept the place clean. It could've been worse.

We didn't talk about Znojmo again. I plotted in silence, knowing the only way was to go back & meet my father on his own ground, face to face. But I couldn't. Weeks dragged by into routine. April became May. The old communists marching in the streets. Star-crossed lovers making poetry on Petřín hill. Not everything changes with the seasons. The women with Walpurgisnacht eyes haunting street corners. White line paranoia for sale in doorways. Boy hustlers & soup kitchens reminding that abyss is only ever a step away. Some nights I worked straight through for no more than a couple of hundred crowns. Behind *St Pauli's*, at the Měšťan brewery, they sold bottles at four crowns from a hole in the wall. We'd get drunk sitting in the gutter, sweating into our shirts. Day-labourers. Construction workers. Dockers. Bums. Cripples. No-hopers.

One morning I came back to the room to find my old man there with his belt undone, bare-chest, & Regen on her back, on that stinking horse hair couch, skirt hiked-up & legs apart, a blank faraway look on her face. She stared at me when I came through the door like she'd never seen me before. It was dawn outside, but the room was choked with shadows. A broken-up TV soundtrack wafted from the apartment next door. In the dim light it was like a scene from Rembrandt. The legs of a hung carcass, the yellowed gash of meat streaked with black. Faces starting out of the gloom.

♠

I don't know when it started to dawn on me that nothing was going to work out the way I'd wanted it to. All those hours wrestling dead meat at the abattoir & I still believed there was somewhere more real I had a ticket to. Day in, day out. When did I wake up & know I existed? I used to have this recurring dream, about struggling to cross a river. In the dream there was a long line of men ahead of me trudging up an endless muddy slope, their heads & torsos invisible beneath the bodies of the fathers they carried on their shoulders. Like carcasses on a slaughterhouse line. Each man hoisting his dead weight ever onwards.

When I was a kid, I promised myself that when I grew up I'd be different from everyone else. I'd go through life without regrets. Not end up like my mother did, hanging myself because life was just a dead-end godless nothing. Or like my father, full of bile & hate. I'd have an idea of who I was & stay true to it through thick & thin. Like a marriage vow. It never seemed wrong to think that way. Unsuspecting, that life has a habit of turning everything you believe around, until the simplest thing in the world becomes an Everest.

Regen knew better. She had ideas of her own & her ideas confused me, upsetting my illusions. Through her I began to see how people looked at me. The thoughts going on behind their eyes sizing me up. How they reckoned they could always put one over.

After mum died I'd get angry for no reason. I'd hide in the cool room & hit out at whatever was in reach. The walls, the pig carcasses, making a mess of myself. The cold would eat down into me & I'd feel more powerless than ever. Like a cog in one of my old man's death machines. I started wishing the bastard would fall down drunk into the teeth of one of them, spewed back out in worms of thick, bloodied mince. But I knew it would never happen. He'd die in his sleep one night, an older man than I'd ever be, his conscience at peace with itself.

Regen told me once about how, in primitive tribes, people would try to get rid of their pain by beating a tethered goat. A scapegoat, she called it. When everything you can see's violent & futile, you try to pass it off onto someone or something else. *Anything* else. A wall, a carcass. You take an object & fill it up with all your hate & bury it somewhere no-one's ever supposed to find it.

I used to think about that sometimes in the wrecker's yard, our secret place, our haven. Like the old bathtub out in the vineyard, it was a kind of lifeboat on a hostile sea. Lying with Regen there beside me, touching me, her words in my ear. I thought about her constantly. Fantasised about the time when we'd be free. I fantasised about her even while we fucked. Her voice, like a voice you hear in dreams, pouring over me, through me, giving form to a shapelessness within. Thoughts I was barely conscious of. Deadly thoughts.

Murderous thoughts. But she taught me patience, also. Deliberation. She ordered the chaos. Defined purpose. Except that revenge is never the thing it seems.

# 10
## NUESTRA SEÑORA DE LA PAZ

You have to learn to use time, instead of trying to kill it. Blake told me that, walking the streets of La Paz, cocaine dialling his mind into a higher state. As he walked, he created. He moved through the crowd like the shadow of a rope dancer. With a word he made the fields & terraced hillsides. Dropping a reed blossom, he made water flow.

The market stalls as we passed them spilled over with the smell of raw meat, goat stomachs, chicken feet. Last days of the wet season.

We'd met by chance, at the second class bus station. He was leaning against the wall beside a payphone, scanning the crowd. I heard his voice before I saw who it belonged to.

"Hey, *muchacho*." A hand coming out from the shadows. I flinched. But instead of a knife, it held a cigarette. "Tienes fuego?" I picked it for a sucker move, shoulders tense. The crowd was blocking the exit. He shook his head, showing his teeth.

I mumbled something & tried to edge away.

"Ty vole!" he laughed, pulling an American lighter from his shirt pocket & snapping a flame out of it. He took a long drag & scrutinised me through slit eyes before he exhaled, blowing smoke in my face. "Your Spanish stinks, *muchacho*. You talk like a goddamn Slovak."

♠

Blake made it his business to ride over to the bus station every other day, to size up the new arrivals, the girls from the coca fields of Chapare. The militias were cracking down on the growers, muscling them out. Refugee kids streamed into the city slums. Blake hustled like a pimp. Flesh-trading.

My instinct was to stay clear. It was the right one, but I didn't. The very thing that set my mind in flight attracted me. Something about him, some signal, some immediate sense of danger. Not that I was afraid of him. I was afraid of myself. Something deep down inside me, something I'd glimpsed the night Regen disappeared.

I'd been running ever since then. First Hamburg. Night train up the river. Border cat-&-mouse. And from Hamburg in a merchant ship to Veracruz. The vast oceanic sense of my predicament. It closed in on me like a prison cell. Fingers tapping against the bulkheads – the many-headed beast of insomnia – a whirlpool at the end of the night, waiting to drag you down into the depths – a gaping mouth cropped out with teeth.

In Veracruz I lay in a cubicle room drinking myself unconscious, expecting at any moment to have my throat slit. Visions of naked-lightbulb desperation. Drifting through a bleak, monstrous fog. Sobered up long enough to hitch a bus west through Zapatista country, military checkpoints. In Tapachula, hustled on the zócalo. Learnt to use a knife. Learnt that when you commit a crime, you'd better know what you're doing. Smuggled cross-border. Big ugly kid. Dark ancient Tartar blood. Black hair, slit eyes, ungainly. *Maricón.* Slept in the markets among the dogs. Camouflage.

My throat itched all the way south to Panama City, Trujillo, Moquegua. Drank to find a still-point, without ever getting there. To dissolve the floors of memory. The flaws of memory. Stealing from life-post to life-post. Multiplying my petty crimes. On the other side of time, a face leered after me, blood in its eyes. Demon of nightmares. Supai. Death god of

67

the ancient Incas. God of sacrificed children. God of insatiable hunger. I could hear everywhere the swarms closing in. The swarms in the waves of the sea. In the wind. In the hollow chasm of the ear.

A toss of a coin put me on a bus to La Paz. The treacherous road inland from the coast, the mountain road winding & winding. Black serpent through hot jungle. Black serpent, eyes afire, twisting & thrashing. Brain-juice fermenting deep down in its gut – spleen, gall bladder, pancreas. Coiling down through primitive invertebrate nauseas. The road turns & turns. Spewed-out onto the altiplano. I drink & it turns. The earth turns under it. The moon over the high cordillera. Over grey scrubland strewn with trash. Egg-like. Irregular. Cracking open. A snake's head forcing itself out.

♠

"The world," Blake said, "is the great educator." He named himself after a dead poet. A madman. An evangelist of the son who kills the father & becomes the father. A naked revolutionary in the garden of earthly delights. "Only in vice & weakness," his voice said, "are men born equal. In the free world, every man's a gaoler & every man's in a prison of his own making. Democracy? The freeman disdains his freedom. He'd rather set himself in chains. Never forget, it's us or them."

Like a *guerillero* retreating to the last outposts of sanity in a war against the mass dream, Blake drifted. He did everything & nothing. He raped & pillaged. He survived. He went all the way down & made it back out.

"The ethics of history is man himself. But ethics, or art, like a man, can be broken & twisted & snuffed-out." So said Blake. I tried to imagine him in a secret police cell under

Bartolomějská street. A pillowcase over his head doused with piss. Cigarette burns. Rubber hose. Refusing to confess his crime. Which alone was his crime.

Blake was no hero. He survived on instinct. Opportunity. Paradox. Shovelling shit wasn't the worst thing that could happen to a man. He took one look at me at the bus station in La Paz & laughed. "Ty vole!" The small woman behind the ticket counter watching us under heavy eyelids. A large Hispano-Olivetti beside her. Breasts under white cotton blouse sagging on folded arms. Two sunburnt foreigners talking gibberish.

"How old are you?" he asked, out on the street. But he cut himself short. "Forget it," he said. "Who gives a fuck how old anyone is. You live, shit & die. And any day short of the last is old enough. May as well take what you can. This place is full of kids who've run away from something. Orphans, a lot of them. Grist for El Alto," pointing through the rain at the sprawl.

La Paz was built at the bottom of a canyon, high up on a plateau. El Alto is the slum spilling over the rim. A bleak hillside of raw concrete, corrugated iron & sheet plastic. A proletarian warren of brothels, coke dens & militia hold-outs owned by somebody. *Nuestra Señora de la Paz*. Our Lady of Peace. Blake lived in the border zone, a mile above the city, in a room in the courtyard of an old infirmary. A dead tree stuck up through the floor. Rain cascaded through the roof. Flies asleep everywhere. He shared the place with a growing tribe of old women & whores. They traded on the kids he brought from the station. He worked them in, looked after them for a while, passed them on. I thought of Regen. *St Pauli*. The *Ace of Spades*. Dead thoughts.

Justification was never part of Blake's game. "Never apologise," he said. "And never explain." Said I had to work my mind if I didn't want to end up in the hole. I'd made do with chance. Slow anger. Mind of an ox. I tried not to stand out. Shrunk down into myself. People looked through me, like there was something they didn't want to see. This big ugly shape bearing over them.

I can't remember how I ended up living in that room, in the old infirmary above La Paz. I was always looking for somewhere to hide. To go numb.

♠

In the frozen late December rain, we rode in a taxi through narrow streets. People thronged around the cantinas, firelight glowing on faces leering from doorways. Blake stopped the taxi at different places along the way. Buying. Selling. Cutting deals. We waited at a bodega for someone he knew. One of his connections. We drank dark Brazilian rum. There was a girl, pregnant, maybe six months, with green plastic sandals & a blanket, sitting on a crate inside the doorway, a basket full of cheap umbrellas at her feet. Part of her skirt tucked between her knees to stop it from getting wet. Blake said something to her. Then the connection arrived. Money changed hands. When we left, the girl came too.

The girl had a name I couldn't remember. Blake knew her. The infirmary, when we finally got there, was a derelict colonial pile teetering on the brink behind a high wall. The wall was covered in old torn-up election posters & graffiti. Broken bottle-glass cemented on top. Downstairs it was quiet. Blake led us through half-a-dozen rooms to the converted courtyard. Light filtered down from an upstairs balcony. Music.

The girl with the green sandals sat on a mattress on the floor with her basket of umbrellas while Blake kicked on some jazz & laid out a dozen lines on an old writing desk. I stood there taking in the surroundings, feeling generally out of place. The girl gave me a vague look, the way you look at something you don't really see. If it weren't for my face, I'd probably be invisible. It's not distinctive, or the cops would've had a field day with me, but it's ugly. An ugliness you don't forget even if you can't describe it.

I'd arrived from the coast with nothing but the ratty Mexican suit I was wearing. A passport. A razor. A stash sewn into my boots. I'd left a bag & a book in a hotel room in Trujillo. Nothing much in the bag but dirty linen. The book was a sheaf of yellow dog-eared pages held together by a thick red elastic band. I remember it because it had no name & it was the first book I'd ever read from beginning to end, though it never seemed to finish. It was about everything & nothing. For a while I found in words the emptiness & silence I'd searched for in the bottle. But it wasn't enough. What the words merely communicated, I needed to become.

"Welcome to La Paz," Blake said. "Make yourself at home." I took a plastic fold-up chair that was upturned in a corner & sat on it. The place stank of mould & dead cigarettes. I leaned back & waited. Blake snorted. "You've got to try this shit," he said, shaking his head. "Better than anything money can buy." He passed a rolled-up dollar bill. I did a couple of lines & he was right.

The girl yawned. She was barely more than thirteen. Blake said something & she put her basket aside & turned around on her knees, the mattress sagging beneath her. There wasn't any ceremony. He lifted her skirt, undid his fly, spat on his cock & fucked her. The girl picked her teeth the whole time. When he finished he went back to the desk to do a couple of more lines. Jerked his head at me to take a turn with the girl & walked out, singing as he did:
*I love you my little child*

*Your eyes are two salt statues*
*That melt like a beautiful day*
*In the hollow of anyone's hand.*

There were voices in the corridor. Laughter. The girl looked over her shoulder at me. She had a face like a million others. Asked if she could do it lying down this time. Her back ached. She spread herself out on the mattress, skirt gathered up in folds beneath her paunch. I thought of the dumb life taking form within her. Afterwards, Blake peals off a couple of American dollars. "For the kid." She seemed to accept all this with calm dignity. Bored. He stroked her head. We went back outside. Left the girl in the street. A few blocks down, Blake led the way through a gate into a garage with a fire burning in a halved 40 gallon drum. The garage was full of people watching a football game on a television in the corner. A woman in an apron came & went, bringing food on plastic trays. Fried plantain. Salteñas. Humitas. Fritanga. Chicharrón. Boys trading cigarettes & booze. Singani. Pisco. Stale tobacco smoke. Quechua voices.

♠

Things continued this way. We drank. Rode taxis. Cruised the bars. The purpose was fixed. A type of nihilistic rationale presided over everything. Months slipped by. The sun at altitude, razor-edged. The wind off the altiplano. I stumbled drunk from one night into the next, a carnival effigy. Another year of my sentence passed. I felt nothing, watching the dark-eyed Aymara girls. Daughters of conquistador slavery. Knee-high boots, dancing the Entradas. Los Caporales. Las Morenadas. Midnight behind the street markets. Parted thighs & mouths. We were descending into the time of Pachakuti. White noise chaos. Sleepless for weeks on end, strung out on coke. Smoke coiling from a cigarette, a girl's blue ribbon, unconsciously caressing it.

Time began to lose its meaning. A sickness had taken hold of me. The mindless carnival turned ugly. I sat in the room & stared at a crack in the wall. I watched it, day & night. Sometimes voices came from the other side of it. Lights. Whispers. The infirmary filled with strangers. Men with machetes, fresh from Chonchoroco. There was violence brooding in the north, in the east. The militias were burning the villages.

"Pity them," Blake said, "praying for someone to save them. The benign white god. General Banzer promises the little children democracy. But the Aymara have been slaves for centuries. Democracy's just a word that's pornographic & cheap."

Blake preached revolt. Wirakocha. Dead trickster eyes. More men came. Often he'd leave with them, a traveller camouflaged in rags. Disappear for days on end then re-emerge in cocaine purgatory, face shrunken around his skull, eyes bulging. Eventually he didn't come back. Nobody paid me any attention. The old women, the whores. I withered into myself, pulp & flesh. I slept. Time passed. A flash of light. Time stood still. I dreamed. Wild fever dreams. Gunfire across the terraces. The air boiling. When I opened my eyes again, my mother was hanging in the tree in the middle of the room. An ecstatic fixity of expression on her face. I sat there listening to the flies as her corpse revolved slowly at the end of its rope.

# 11
## TEMPLE OF LOST SOULS

At the end of the nightmare, someone's watching me. I know this as I knew it then. The spirit in the dark, behind the eyes, that sees everything I see & sees me also. In La Paz, Blake drove me like an alter-ego. I'd already gone to the bottom of the night & he led me deeper. "We live by extremes," he said. "The rest is suicide, by the other means." Where Regen taught patience, Blake taught excess. To know, to kill, to create. But there were no verbs in what he conjugated. Blake dealt by stolen language left incomplete, significations of mutual cruelty, chaos & derangement. And like every teacher, he was a myth.

Lying there in the courtyard in the infirmary, I couldn't tell how long I'd been alone. I stared for hours at the phantom hanging in the tree until it seemed a fog inside my mind cleared. Then, sitting beneath the tree, I saw there was a boy. He had Blake's eyes, I thought, as if it were a sign. When he noticed I was looking at him he stood & motioned for me to get up. I struggled. A smell of death came off me, like nail varnish. I swayed & only just managed to stay on my feet. After a while the room stopped spinning & the tree stood still.

The boy led me through the weirdly empty building to the scullery. There was water in a cistern & I drank from it like a man dying of thirst. The water threw up strange reflections. I felt the growth on my face. The slack, wax-like flesh. My eyes ached. I only wanted to sleep, but the boy wouldn't let me. I could hear voices from some distant place. A rhythmic pounding on barred doors. The boy led me down into the cellar, in an impenetrable darkness. He lit a candle that danced & flickered off stone walls thick with slime. A tunnel veered off into nothingness. I stumbled & crawled. I felt a long tether dragging me along an infinite slope.

When daylight came again, we were somewhere in the El Alto sprawl. All around us, the scent of erupting violence. Distant plumes of tear gas. Echoes of gunfire. There was no rest. We pushed through the streets until the boy somehow conjured a taxi out of the throng. I watched faces blur through the taxi window. The journey was a depthless strip of blackened film punctuated by flaring lights, disconnected landscapes, unknown people, fever & brain sickness.

From La Paz we drifted north to Cobija. Across salt flats, mountains, lunar valleys. A man on the side of the road, beside a festering donkey. A truck with soldiers leaning out of it, lazily sweeping the scenery with their guns. We passed across the yawning, barren altiplano & the oceanous lakes. Vast stretches of delirium beneath an unrelenting sun. The red calligraphic disc of the heat at dusk. The room in the old infirmary travelled with me. In my mind it became smaller & smaller until, like the sun, it was the size & colour of a plum. A plum with a blackened stalk stuck up out of it & a shrivelled leaf hanging down. I swallowed it whole. The room became me. The corpse. The tree. I no longer knew if any of it was real. It didn't have to be. It was an emblem. A mark on my burnt forehead. A third eye. A talisman.

The fever never left me. It varied only in intensity. Paranoia. Fear & trembling. From Cobija, across the border & the brown turbid waters of the Rio Acre into Brazil. Vine-entangled jungle paths. North. North-west. West. A demon with Blake's eyes led me on. Night after night through frenzied landscapes. Then another border & a town called Contamana. And then jungle again. Struggling to keep a foothold. Telling myself I didn't have the legs for it any more, if only I could lie down & sleep or die. But always another voice, hissing in my ear, driving me on, counting the steps.

We followed the Rio Ucayali, mind swimming in the vacuum left by the body in its absence. There were no more paths, every direction was the same, only the river distinguished one from another. I wandered in incomplete circles, each time ending face-down in water. The demon boy vanished inside my reflection.

Bit by bit my fever gave birth to horrors, bleeding out of me. The jungle heaved. Night caved in, telescoping through a hole in the world. On the other side, a room, a shanty on a river bank. The jungle seemed to fill it up. Howler monkeys, parrots, lizards, spiders gleaming on their webs. Fruit rotted on the floor among empty bottles. Mango, papaya, guanabana. I lay there, boa constrictor eyes staring down from dead branches. A voice spoke to me. "Once upon a time," the voice said, without ever getting any further. Over & over & over again. Beginning but never continuing, as though waiting for me, like a child, to tell it the words that must come next.

♠

Somewhere a man is doubled up, vomiting shit all over himself. Watery shit oozing from his mouth, dribbling down his chin. He looks so pathetic there. A crumpled sack of a man. Barely recognisable. Barely a man. But I still know him. He's me.

We're on a boat. A canoe. On a river. It could be anywhere. The whole continent stretches out around us in its uncreated chaos. And yet something about this place, this time, must've been preordained. The laughing god drawing a circle in the dust with a sharpened bone. We're in the middle of the jungle. Air humid, thick with insects, piranhas stirring the water. Adrift, moving with the tide, onwards & onwards, for days, weeks, months, years.

He's lying at stern, knotted up on himself, a spasm of human meat. A thick carpet of flies covers his face. A red hole of a mouth. Crust of dried retchings. He lies there & I watch him dying. When I'm not watching him, I sleep. When I don't sleep, I wait. I no longer perform bodily functions, I'm merely a pair of eyes, a pair of hands.

The Swiss who sold us the canoe was almost blind. A Lutheran missionary on the Rio Ucayali – last outpost on the trail into the abyss. The canoe was old & needed calking. While the dying man sat & stared at the river, I calked. I bought wood to raise the sides. To fix a mast. Awning cloth to rig a makeshift sail. Bartered strips of cured monkey meat from the indios. Bartered the dying man's shoes. His belt. A canvas bag with an old double-barrelled shotgun, a few charts, a compass, twenty-one dollars in Ecuadorian currency. There was an old camera, too. A Nikon F2 manual. Antique. I asked the half-blind missionary to take a picture of the two of us together, beside the canoe – me holding the dying man up. Out on the river, I dropped the camera overboard. Our images like two genies in a bottle sunk in the river bed. A temple for lost souls.

♠

The dying man arrived one day out of the Ecuadorian jungle, just like I had, only from the opposite direction, coming south. He was alone. Face peeling, a stringy three-week's growth. He looked the way I'd looked weeks earlier. Intestines melting down. Putrefying & fermenting. Fear eating the pancreas. Duodenum, jejunum, ileum. Malarial brain unravelling from pylorus to anus. Waves of backwards peristalsis. Bile & shit. Vomiting.

I stare at the photograph in the dying man's passport until it becomes as familiar as a face in a mirror. United by accident. By chance. Providence. Destiny. I say his name to myself for hundreds of hours on end, learning it. Learning to become it. Divining its inner life. I wait for him to die. I wait deliberately. This, I whisper to myself, is salvation. A gift horse. A second life.

On & on we drift. Past the silhouettes of ocean-going ships, two thousand miles inland. On & on, through the long night of the soul. I hear him gasp. Last voice. Last breath. I stuff my own tattered passport inside his shirt. He's me now. We drift against the riverbank. Cicadas, frogs, mosquitoes. A whole requiem. I drag the corpse onto land, prop it against a tree stump where maybe one day someone'll find it. Stir an ant nest underfoot. Cast off into the river's vastness.

I watch the shit-stained face dissolve into gloom, becoming him now. Being him. Raised up like Lazarus from the dead:

*I am the resurrection & the life.*
*He who believes in me will live, even though he dies.*
*And whoever lives & believes in me will never die.*

♠

Writ on the evolutionary scale, each purpose cancels out the other. Like justice or liberty, set in stone, cast iron, blood & bone. The day comes & you slip out into the open, breathing the air. A sweet, fetid perfume. The world is this great big rotten fruit, spewing forth countless species in mortal contest. We vanquish, we decimate. Yet time remains closed. The enemy is always within. We remain that toy of paradox, to mythify smallest actions, a colossus in the jungle whose head is a room for a midget to grow old in.

I lie in the seepage at the bottom of the canoe, alone now, night bulging, remote cities spread across the sky. Pinpricks of light. Imagine future life, other worlds. Man-in-space: tin can floating down rivers of time into the big nothing. Black hole metaphysics. Strange constellations rear their monstrous heads. Monkey faces, piranha-mouthed. Night's canopy spreads out across the eye's infinity.

Hours stretch into days into weeks. Up the winding river, through floodplains, into the Amazon. Iquitos. Orosa. Chichita. Nameless villages invisible through the foliage. Outposts obscured across the river's breadth. A plateau of brown & black water stretching away like Siberian steppes. Huge port cities rearing up out of the flatness. Dense tracts of submerged forest fringing the tide.

As I lie there with the river under me & the sky above me, I try to imagine seeing through the dead man's eyes. I pronounce the heavy guttural speech of the dead man's language. A language which I've somehow known since childhood. *Der Fluss zum Himmel. Der Himmel über dem Fluss.* Our histories merge within the slowly turning currents, the sweep of river debris pulled along inexorably to the sea.

♠

Once again I'm lying in the old bathtub out in the vineyards. Up in the sky the clouds are shape-shifting against the blue. A red kite dangling a long tail winds in & out of view & appears infinitely far away. What would it be like up there flying alongside it, weightless, high above the world? The tide rocks under me & the world shifts. It's Autumn. If I concentrate hard I can picture the men in the fields. Bundles of vine wood heaped up for the bonfire that'll soon mark the end of the harvest season & the start of *vinobraní* – the

*Weinlesefest.*

Long trestle tables are set out in the courtyard. Fat loaves of *šumava*. Wheels of stinking *tvarůžky*. Soon the first *burčák* begins to flow straight from the barrel. It fizzes in the mouth like baking soda & sours fast. Everyone who's worked the harvest teeters around the barrel ritually gulping it down like fish gulping air. By divine edict, all & sundry duty-bound to get filthy drunk. Elbows work with an almost Presbyterian fury. And while the *burčák*'s being swilled, the local pig farmer drags in a prime sow & they slit its throat. Hang it from a hook over the barn door & gut it. Whoosh! The blood drained into a tub for black pudding. Three groans for piggy-wig.

By evening, when the pig's well & bled, they light the bonfire. The drunks stand around leering at the flames, howling like monkeys. After the fire settles down the pig's skewered on a spit & roasted slowly over the coals. Then the music begins. The bowsies sing & dance. From time to time someone prods the carcass with a stick & ladles fat over the crisped meat. All the local brats come to watch. They hide under the tables, scoffing *burčák*, sick as parrots. Nobody cares.

I'm lying in the old bathtub & Regen's lying there beside me, watching the stars & listening to the shitfaced couples rutting in the dark among the vines. The bonfire glow turns the shadows into a wild moth-dance spiralling up through the night, flaring into starburst. I think how beautiful it would be to lie there with Regen forever. Free to invent the world. To own the sunrise. To sail ahead of the great deluge, bathed in warm orange light. But somewhere above the crazed music, the laughter & drunken voices, there's a droning that gets louder & more insistent until it hangs over us like the shadow of a great oppressive black bird, eclipsing everything.

# 12
## RIOJA

The city falls away beneath us. Standing on the great pediment, swaying in the half-drunk gloom. Wind in our faces. The river glistens. White flash of gulls swooping & falling. And all of this but a moment's reprieve? The girl from the *Marquis de Sade* is still beside me. Inessa. A name. Any name would do. We watch the city's drama unfold. Sirens & streetlights, the razzle-dazzle cortège. Her hand touching mine. I feel her shiver, pull her close. Face lost in the dead metronome's shadow.

Crossing the blacked-out terraces. Tree skeletons swaying. We meet people's shadows in the streets, grown dark in mid-winter afternoon. It's barely four o'clock. The motionless theatres of storefront windows. Stockinged mannequins. Furs. Objects staring out of painted eyes. A shop assistant kneeling, drawing a black lace in & out of the eyelets of a woman's shoe. Advertisements for a life reduced to something anyone could understand. Love, pain, happiness.

Tram windows flash past like the frames of a film.

Inessa, sloe-eyed, presses against me in my oversized Gestapo coat. I, with my undertaker's suit, grown thin under the weather. Nobody pays us any attention. Two characters in a wrong film. The film we all imagine ourselves in but are constantly vanishing from. A man & a woman with no past. Two figments. Two strangers. As anonymous to one another as they are to the world.

♠

Traffic surges at the intersection. People on the sidewalk rushing somewhere, talking, doing nothing, waiting, huddled against the cold. We cross Letenské Square to a narrow street even darker than the ones before. Dead leaves mulched into pavement. A jutting neon sign above stairs leading down. We push through a heavy red door into a basement tapas bar. A blanket of warm air enfolds us. Cigarette smoke cut-through with char-grill & hashish. We find a corner table, ease down under the low lighting. The place is all moody sensuous, walls painted deep scarlet lake. Inessa ditches the coat, slides out of the black turtle neck, a black singlet over pale skin. I let my eyes wander all over her. Long neck, small breasts, collar bones standing out. She leans over & picks something off the floor.

Just then a waitress in a Spanish dress comes to the table. Black hair pulled back tight, hoop earrings. Wide hazel eyes. I try to make a smile, but the waitress doesn't smile back. I order wine. Food. Inessa looks at me questioningly, says nothing.

"Don't worry," I tell her. "Everything's good here."

Outside it starts raining, heavier than before. The waitress returns with a bottle of red & sets it down between us. Rioja. Tempranillo. Returns again with bowls of green & black olives, grilled peppers, anchovies, bread. Flamenco music broods in the background, a guitar making unrequited love to the rain. A couple on the other side of the bar are dancing, slow.

I pour some wine, raise my glass. Inessa's still looking at me. She lays something down on the table in front of her. A folded square of paper. I tip the glass back, pour more wine.

"What is it?"

She unfolds the paper. It's the picture Blake gave to me. The picture of the dead girl. It must've slipped out of the coat pocket where I'd forgotten it. I stare at the dead girl's face. It seems so long ago already, I barely recognise it. The rest of her's not a pretty sight.

"She's dead," I say, as if it wasn't obvious enough already. "I was at the morgue this morning. A friend took that. A photographer." As though that explained anything. Why I'd kept it. Why she'd had to find it. Like there's some sort of programme to these things.

"Who is she?"

"Nobody knows."

Inessa looks thoughtfully at the creased photograph for a moment, tracing the autopsy stitches with her fingernails. The paper's fold-marks neatly cut the body in four parts, centred at the groin.

"Somebody knows," she says. Words like déjà vu.

"Sure," I say. "Somebody always knows."

I finish the glass of wine I'm holding & pour another. I finish that too & then empty the bottle. On cue the waitress comes over & asks if we want another one. I nod. She glances sidelong at the photograph & goes away. A little paler, it seems. Inessa looks across at me, her face a complex of unreadable emotions.

"How did she die?"

"They say she drowned."

"They say?"

"What do I know, I never saw the girl before in my life."

"And these?" she asks, pointing at the rope marks.

Something comes over me then. I put my face in my hands & try to rub out the picture. I tell myself again it's not *her*. Wondering what I'm doing *here*. All the lies I've had to become. But she doesn't know anything. Inessa. She's just a kid from a bar.

I tell her what I know. What I think I know. It isn't

83

much. Just the story. The way it might've come out in the evening news. DEAD GIRL FOUND IN RIVER. But even as I'm telling it I'm thinking about Blake. He *knew* her. He'd photographed her while she was alive. It's the only way any of it made sense. The rope marks. Him bribing the stiff at the morgue. Me as his witness. His accomplice. His alibi.

The idea's sick. I feel my guts turn over, a shiver runs the length of my spine. My neck's all wet. I'm rigid. Staring hard at the black space in front of me. Inessa's voice brings me out of it. My face does something ugly, I can see it in her expression. I know then that I'm just as ugly on the outside as I am on the inside. I expect her to get up & run while she's got the chance, but she doesn't. Instead she reaches across the table & touches my cheek. I feel confused.

"Look at me," she says. I struggle not to, but her gaze holds onto me, a piercing azure. "Tell me what it is."

I shake my head. I don't want to go there. I'm saved by the waitress who brings another bottle & sets it down on the table. The picture's still lying there but she avoids looking at it. When she's gone I reach over & pick it up, turning it so that I can see everything. It doesn't affect me this time. I tell myself it's not anything real, it's just an image.

"Did *you* know her?"

I fold the picture & slip it inside my suit jacket. I think for a moment, weighing my words. Then decide to say what I wasn't going to say.

"I knew someone like her. It was a long time ago."

♠

We're sitting at a corner table. The rain rat-tat-tats on casement windows. It's later. Much later. Rain has a way of rearranging time. Like being in the past & looking towards the present the way you look across a room at someone coming towards you. Other rooms at other times. Faces or the absence of them – the ones you fear or the ones you expect. Saying there are things too precious to be allowed to be forgotten. A whole existence embroidered out of lies, so that I'll never have to return there, to any of those places.

Inessa keeps her eyes averted as she listens. Words interwoven with the sound of the rain. Counterpoint. Darkness & light. I'm telling her the story of Regen. Like a wind-up drunk singing his only tune, out of tune. I don't know why I'm doing it except that I know it's not for her sake. Once upon a time I had people to blame for my life not making any sense. The hardest thing to walk away from is an alibi you don't *need* anymore.

I tell Inessa the story of a child who had her childhood stolen from her, & then everything else stolen from her. If you make it general enough it could be anyone's story. It occurs to me as I'm telling it, that it could be Inessa's, too. Prague's full of girls from Russia, Ukraine, Moldova who end up tied into the business. White slavery. Life-time bondage to the smugglers who got them here.

They start out in the brothels & strip joints off Wenceslas Square & slowly get used up. Bit by bit sliding down the scale into the rotation system, from one sleaze pit to another, winding up on the border, the E55, or working the streets around Můstek, Hlavní Nádraží, Libeň. A few get lucky as call girls. Maybe wind up making it on the porn circuit, too. But you can't stop time & sooner or later the goods get well & tainted, & each new gig means more for less, harder, filthier, more vicious. Till they wind up like the dead girl maybe with a rope around their necks being tortured in front of a camera by snuff freaks.

# 13

## LA FIN DU MONDE

There's a bar off rue Mouffetard in Paris, called *La Fin du Monde*. The end of the world. It doesn't seem so long ago, the train from Le Havre, Blake's atelier, the night of the Spaniard. Just like old times. La Paz. The infirmary on the hill. The mad room with the dead tree sticking up through the floor. Waking on the Place de la Contrescarpe, slumped beneath a lamppost clutching my duffel bag. I thought, I'd got so far but still hadn't made it home & probably never would. Though for what it's worth, still in one piece. More or less.

I mustn't have been asleep there long, but it was dawn already, voices along the street. I hoiked up a gob of bloodied phlegm & spat. Raw behind the eyes. I'd been sick by degrees since I boarded that first ship out. The rest was just a kind of refinement. Like the stamp collection every kid keeps under his bed.

I was halfway down rue Mouffetard when I noticed *La Fin du Monde* with its shutters up. I staggered in & leaned against the bar. A drunk in the corner was humming a tune to himself that could've been anything at all or nothing. I dug in my pockets for loose change & spilled what I had on the counter. The barman glanced at it with his one good eye, unimpressed. The other eye was fogged glass with something swimming in it. I asked for a brandy. He poured a *demi* & left it in front of me. Then pointed at my face. There was dried blood on my cheek, probably from a fight with that lamppost.

"Cops beat up some Arab kids last night."

"Sure," I said. "The cops are always beating up on someone."

I tried to remember what'd happened the night before. Faces leering through brain fog. Blake, sitting there in that bar in the Marais exactly as if it'd been arranged. Perhaps he'd never left. Perhaps he'd been with me all along. Like a shadow. At one moment there ahead of me, at the next silently stalking me. Invisible. Anticipating me with every step. Mephistopheles-like.

"Don't know what's good for 'em," the barman grunted.

"You said it. Nothing like a boot in the arse to give a kid an education."

He looked at me trying to catch on if I meant something by it. Figured I didn't & wiped a dirty rag along the counter.

"Boot in the arse is too good for some. Want it handed on a platter. You know," he hung the rag over his shoulder, "when I was a kid, people did like they were told."

I knocked back the drink & pushed myself away from the counter.

"Yeah? What were you told?"

He grinned sideways, sliding the empty glass towards the slops in the sink.

"Travail, Famille, Patrie!" his right hand thumping his chest. "Nowadays," he croaked, "nothing's worth a damn. You'll wake up one day with your throat slit." Casually he popped his glass eye & started polishing it with the rag, moving his jaw side-to-side as he did. A couple more drunks stumbled in from the street. Workers in grease-smeared blue overalls. "Mark my word," the barman hissed. One of the drunks slapped the bar & called for a drink. "What's the rush," the barman called back, thumbing his glass eye into its socket. "Mark my words," he said again, slapping the dirty rag against the counter.

87

"Ricard!" the drunk shouted, holding up two fingers. Like it was the barman's name, & he should go stuff himself. I shouldered my bag & hit the street. *Travail, Famille, Patrie.* Work, family, fatherland. The Hail Mary of fascist scum everywhere. If it meant anything more than a license to beat a population into submission, I didn't know what it was. As far as I could see, the price of minding your own business is a kick in the crotch. It's that kind of world.

♠

The place I grew up in doesn't exist anymore. The orchards cut down, vines uprooted, the fields overgrown. The vineyard with the old bathtub where I made love to Regen for the first time. The tree my mother hanged herself from. I might just as well have dreamed it all. Those figments out of which grow the landscapes of childhood, standing out like a ruin in bas-relief. It was as if a part of reality had disappeared.

How long had I been away? Things happen in ten years. Things build, things dissolve. It was October the last time I went back there, searching for the house Regen used to live in. The train station at Božice looking the way it always had. The name painted on the sign above the awning of the station house. It looked ridiculous there, after all this time. God's backwater. God the non-existent.

I took the same groaning old blue & white bus out past the meatworks. The meatworks outlined against the sky like the crenellated rubble of a toppled fortress, jutting out from some remote place & time. Where Regen's house had been there was nothing but foundation blocks. The farm buildings, abandoned. Windows smashed, floorboards torn up, all weeds & nettles. The matted remains of dead pigeons lay strewn about the ground.

The bus driver said they'd sold up. The house had been knocked down for a bypass that ran out ten miles before it ever got there. A pair of concrete bridges stood in the middle of the fields, like bits of ancient aqueduct. A smashed winepress stuck up above the grass. I stood there, rooted, staring at it. Ants covered my shoes. A hot wind rustling the tall grass. The sound of bees mourning their lost hives.

I don't know what I'd expected to find. The world at a standstill & everything the way it once seemed it'd always been. I'd hitchhiked back to Prague from Porte d'Orléans, exhausted & sick. I slept on a mattress in the back of a truck all the way to Strasbourg. Then crossed Germany on the E50. It took two days to get to Prague, dozing on the roadside for an hour at a time.

In Prague I waited, looking for signs. People who might've remembered me, people who wouldn't. I found a gig babysitting a scrapheap on the river. It suited me. No-one asked questions. I could keep an eye on things. Fill in the blanks. I watched people come & go from *St Pauli's*. I staked out the old dives. Some of the places weren't there anymore. The names changed. Buildings stripped out for redevelopment. I went through the phonebook. Nothing. Registry offices. Missing persons. I spent hour after hour standing on Libeňský bridge, watching the greybrown waters churn. The last place I'd seen Regen, standing in the rain on a late August night. Trying to summon her ghost.

Ten years of wanting to believe that everything which ends begins again. That nothing's ever final. That what's taken can be taken back. Night after night listening in my mind to the low regular sound of Regen breathing beside me. Brown light through a window. Her clenched fists as she slept. And somewhere, in a dark place the eye can't see, the shape of my vengeance. A warm voluptuous shape, swollen with hatred.

I wanted the story to complete itself. I'd spent months, years, looking for all the connections. The loose threads. The contradictions. I held the image of Regen in my mind & the more I held her the more remote she seemed. I searched my memory. Struggled to keep the delusions at bay. The nightmare faces. Jungle paranoias. I charted maps of her secret existence. Consulted spirits. Read many books. Bided my time.

♠

It was less than a month after I'd returned to Prague that Blake tracked me down. It wasn't hard. He knew enough of my story to know I wouldn't be far from the scene of the crime. I was sitting on a green plastic beach chair, on the foredeck of the Greek's barge, with a fishing line cast out in the river, waiting for something to bite. It's a way of passing the time. The fish are no good for eating. The river's toxic – full of dioxins & heavy metals – but not quite enough to kill the bottom-feeders that suck on the river mud. It's not the kind of place you'd want to take a swim, though plenty have.

The sun was just showing over the tree-tops when Blake rode out of the grey morning on his motorcycle. Face like a kabuki mask, eyes drawn-in, unreal. A black leather jacket with a bulge under the left shoulder. Silver hair standing on end. I looked up from my tackle & found myself staring into a camera lens. Shutter click & whir. He climbed up onto the deck & stood beside me, camera slung around his neck, & took in the scenery.

"Dobré," he said, shaking a cigarette from a packet of Gitanes & lighting it. "Tout va bien, uh?" He picked a shred of tobacco from his teeth. "View could definitely be worse."

The autumn trees had already begun shedding along the riverbanks, but there was still plenty of yellow & red to make the scene into a picture. The barge lay in a brown inlet, with a slipway at one end & a used car lot behind it surrounded by razor wire. The view in the other direction took in the river & a plateau where the Bohnice madhouse was. High-rise communist-era tenements made a grey barricade against the sky.

Something tugged at one of the lines, but it was only a tease. We stared at the water for a while to see what might materialise then gave up & went inside. The gloom below decks immediately enveloped us. Boots on steel rungs. Blake coughed. Flashback to a ship far out at sea. Fog on the water. The low throbbing of the ship's engine. Sound of a ghost crew moving about the companionways. Flashforward to the galley, grey light through portholes illuminating a cut-out menagerie of faces pasted onto the walls.

Blake stubbed out his cigarette, uninterested. I found a half-empty bottle of slivovice on a shelf & some glasses.

"Keeping busy." It didn't sound like a question.

Blake took a chair & sat with his feet crossed on the table, face in the shadows. I poured the brandy. We drank.

"You alone here?"

I shrugged. It was obvious enough. Blake lit another cigarette, blew smoke at the ceiling. We drank some more.

"It's like a submarine," he said all of a sudden, waving his cigarette at the walls. "You know what Freud would've said."

"Do I care?"

"Anyone ever tell you that Freud was a Moravák, like you?"

"Freud was an Austrian Jew is what the books say."

"It's true," he said, rubbing his bottom lip. "He was born in Příbor. His father was a locksmith. Fancy that."

"What's that prove?"

"He committed suicide in London."

"Some people commit suicide, some people just die. Marx died in London."

"Marx was a fraud."

"Freud was a junky. So what?"

"You've got no sophistication, my friend." Blake grinned. His teeth yellow-grey in the half-light. "Do you know what your problem is?"

"No," I said, pouring out more slivovice. "But I bet you didn't come all this way to tell me."

"Your Freud, you know what he said – that every man harbours a secret desire to murder his father & rape his mother."

"No kidding? Any schoolboy could tell you that."

"But not every schoolboy does it," he said.

"Amen."

I stared through the cigarette smoke at Blake's face, barely seeing him at all. Only a shape. An accident of contrasting light.

"The point is, *muchacho*, that we're all just machines," he said, taking the bottle & pouring himself another glass. "All instinct & sex & unconsciousness. It's everything humanity is & does. And everything it *doesn't* do, also." He tipped the glass back. Sat it down on the scratched table top beside the unlabelled bottle. "All of so-called western civilisation's a fucking machine. It began with the evolution of protozoa. In the beginning was the machine, dividing & multiplying. Replicating, mutating, feeding the slime from which our forebears crawled forth, cast off their gills to reinvent themselves as that eating, shitting, killing & fucking machine called humanity. And we act like we invented the idea."

"Since when did you care about civilisation?"

"Do you know what I've found out?" He took in a lungful of smoke & blew it in my face. I waved the smoke away. Stood up & went over to the sink. "God's a machine, too." I wasn't really interested in Blake's philosophy, but that'd never held him back in the past. "A fucking machine, *muchacho*. A *fucking* machine."

I found old coffee grounds & poured lukewarm water from the kettle over them. The result was what you'd expect, but I drank it anyway. The slivovice was beginning to send me to sleep. Or perhaps it was Blake who was sending me to sleep. God & philosophy. Martians. UFOs. What did it matter? We act as we believe, & contradict that also. The world goes on. Nothing pays us any mind.

"When I use *this*," he said, fingering his camera, "it's all there, *inside*. The ghost in the machine. The divine spirit. God, evolution, the cosmos." He laughed too quietly for me to tell the shape of his laughter. "Just like you're a ghost," he went on, still laughing, "inside this boat. Look at you," he said, though I couldn't see his face.

There was a clinking of glass as Blake helped himself to another refill. I stared into the bottom of my empty coffee cup, but there was no-one down there to stare back at me.

# 14
## PROVIDENCE

It feels like a long time since it got dark. Time, like a train whose doors are locked, coursing through the night without ever stopping, without ever reaching a destination. Outside, the world's a shapeless blur sinking into shadow. A thing that can't ever be grasped.

Being alone was never hard for me. I'm what other people call an only child. We both were. I never knew why. My mother said I'd been an accident, as though I should've been grateful for it. But that's what I was, the sum total of my reason for being – an accident. When it comes down to it, you could say everything in the world's an accident. My mother, however, believed in creation, the divine mystery, providence. Had the world not been what it is, she'd never have chosen to *have* me at all. I think of what Regen chose in Znojmo. A dead foetus in a toilet. Could've ended up like that myself. If I keep the image in my mind too long, I see it come alive. Its face animates into expression. Its eyes slit open. And it knows who I am.

But what's there to know? I look at my own reflection & all I experience is a mixture of fear, hate, disgust. Jungle instincts. I know that it doesn't have to be like that, but it is. Something lurking beneath the surface of the night. I used to watch my mother pray to her God, the God of little children, of sacrificial lambs. The God of Abraham. Down on her knees in the dark, hands together, supplicant. Had she but eyes to see the Beast she coupled with. Or did I have the picture wrong? It wasn't like that? It wasn't her?

"Religion," Blake once said, "is for sinners, as morality is for hypocrites."

Well it's easy to act wise. Time, they say, still has a habit of making fools of us. That face in the mirror, distorted out of recognition. After all these years, I've even come to look like him. The father in the son. Should I have mercy on him? Or should I murder him again while I still have the chance?

♠

Had his eyes been knives he would've slashed me to pieces. Rooted in the doorway of the room above *St Pauli's*, hands leaden at my sides. I stood there, cretinised & staring, trapped inside a reflex that wouldn't release me. Regen, lying on the couch, legs spread, watching now with a kind of detached curiosity. They both looked like they were waiting for something to happen. But nothing happened. The gloom deepened. Street sounds filtered through the window. Drunken voices from the brothel below. And then the sound of my father unlooping his belt, in a calm, continuous motion.

The first blow caught me across the throat. I raised my hands, but too late. The blows came one after another, in a dark fury. I staggered as he kicked me. Sunk down into a huddle, arms crossed over my head. He whipped me until my whole back burned & kept whipping me.

I went numb, detached from everything, like an eye floating in the corner of the room. I watched my father bring his knee down between my shoulders & pull my head back by the hair. I felt the belt-leather make a noose. And then he was dragging me down the stairs by the neck. An old woman's shrill voice shouted obscenities from the level above. At the bottom landing the belt loosened. I felt my father's breath against my ear:

"You tragic little cunt."

His footsteps receded back up the stairway. Laughter. The sound of the apartment door closing.

I lay there breathing hard. The minutes passed. It seemed like hours. I pulled myself up from the tiles & sat in the half-dark, my back to the wall. There were noises from above. Remote, indistinct noises.

I'd been drinking before, but now I was sober. I stared at my hands. They seemed wrong, like hands of rubber. I tried to clench my fists, but it didn't work. Thoughts struggled & failed to cohere. The tiles made lopsided patterns on the floor.

Eventually a light came on in the stairwell & then footsteps again. I sat there, unmoving, hands palm-up on my knees like a beggar's. The footsteps came to a halt in front of me. I could see the patterning of the leather workman's boots. Boots I'd known all my life. I waited for the blow, but there was none. Only the jangling of coins spilling across my hands onto the floor & a voice weighted with sarcasm:

"The pleasure was all mine."

♠

The door of the room was open. Regen sat on the edge of the couch with her feet tucked under her. I could read the contempt in her face. She barely looked at me, but when she did it was like sticking long fine needles into my eyes. It seemed like everything should've ended then, but it didn't. Our tale had still some way to go. Little Hans & little Greta – lost in the woods – wolves howling in the night all around us.

There was no choice now but to leave – to find somewhere new where my father couldn't track us down. I suspected Regen's aunt of informing. There were ugly scenes. Regen said nothing. Eventually it occurred to me to go to the one place he'd never suspect. There was an old cottage by the lake near Božice that Regen had often told me about. Someone from her parent's congregation owned it. They used to have picnics out there & go swimming. But the owner had moved to Canada & the place hadn't been visited in years. It was a good bet no-one would be living there. We'd be right in my father's shadow & he'd never know it.

I began plotting my revenge in earnest. Regen watched impassively as I packed our belongings, the little we had, never leaving the couch. How many fuckings had it witnessed in its long career, I wondered, as I stuffed our lives into bags. Saying over & over in my head that the story wasn't meant to end this way & maybe it was up to me after all to rewrite this bit, only I knew good & well there aren't any happy endings in this world. Hänsel & Gretel don't just find their way out of the woods by magic, bearing the dead witch's treasure straight into the arms of their axeman father who really loved them all along. Tears in their eyes. Sound up on violins. Roll credits. *And now for a preview of next week's show.*

It was night already when I crossed the bridge into Libeň & found an old Škoda unlocked outside a bookie joint. Hot-wiring it was easy. Back at *St Pauli's* I crammed everything we owned in the back seat. At first Regen wouldn't leave. Her aunt swore at me. Accused me of pimping Regen on the sly. I thought that was rich coming from her, but she shut up when I shoved a fistful of notes in her face. I could easily have broken the sour bitch's neck, but I'd had enough of my own heroics for one day.

"It's time to go," I told Regen. But she still wouldn't move. I reached down to take her by the hand & she cringed. I said it again & she stood up, keeping a distance. Her movements were jarred, as though she'd frozen up somewhere inside. A mechanism that'd broken. Voicelessly she walked downstairs to the car. I closed the door behind her when she got in, eyes gone dead, staring straight off into nothing. Everything had come to this.

The days & weeks living, if you call it living, in that closet of a room people came each night to fuck in. Trolling the streets for work. Running down. Killing time. And night after night drifting apart, helpless before events we were too innocent or dumb or weak to act against. The dream evaporating, becoming that dull futile resentment that feeds whole under-classes of humanity. Estranged from ourselves & each other. Embarrassed at what I saw myself becoming. Afraid of losing her – Regen – grown more & more remote, like a swimmer caught in an undertow, who you wave at because you can't save.

♠

As I closed the door behind her, staring at the roof of the stolen car, brown under the street lights, an incident came back to me. Something I'd forgotten. How only a couple of mornings previous, it was a Sunday, we were walking through the city after another long night. Exhausted, like the days working the slaughter house, & her there with the scent of disillusionment clinging to her, hand limp in mine.

Crossing Můstek, the five a.m. horrors emerging from Metro exits, pale grey & shivering. I remember looking down at my feet & wondering how the rest of my body stayed attached to them. Regen beside me, sweating inside her skin. We were walking towards the silhouette of the Museum, but the direction seemed arbitrary. In a doorway a hustler was shaking down a drunk who'd pissed himself & couldn't keep his legs. The whores on Wenceslas Square were rigid with abjection. A rigor mortis seemed to have invaded everything as the grey light of dawn leeched away all residual sanctuary the night may have left behind it.

Regen's face when I looked at her was full of disgust. When we got to the top of the square she spat as if to rid herself of some contaminant. I remember laughing, & it struck me how ridiculous we each must've appeared to the other, like creatures from different planets. For a moment longer I stood there just looking at her & laughing, low down inside. I couldn't recognise her anymore. She must've been thinking the same about me, but she wasn't laughing.

And now I could hear that menacing laughter once again. Our lives, everything we had, was broken, the way a thing breaks when you smash it against a wall. I told myself I could put it right, but I couldn't get the sound of that laughter out of my head. As I drove us through the night across Bohemia, the welts rising on my back, I told myself the same thing again & again until I almost believed it. But the laughter in my head only grew more insistent, until I too began to laugh. Quietly at first. A barely audible noise deep down in my throat. Some fatalistic reflex made me start to go over all the things Regen had told me about herself on the long train journey from Znojmo, quietly laughing all the while. Things I'd never known before then. Things I'd never even begun to suspect. Thinking how funny it was now. Dawned on me finally how her life had always been a mystery to me. Imagining, during all that time, something as trite & ridiculous as a love without shadows. And yet even now still clinging to it.

# 15
## SOLITAIRE

Another bar in the same part of town. It's almost ten o'clock. A klezmer trio in zoot suits is wheezing out muted horn-notes & asthmatic accordion sounds like stalled traffic. The place looks like a bazaar, every available piece of wall hung with looted Yiddish junk. A pair of Hanukkah candelabra by the door serving as a coat rack. Fake old-world melancholia draped over everything.

I'm sitting alone in an armchair at a low table with an oil lamp in the middle of it. The armchair's stuffing is spilling out, hanging from the arms in long greasy cords. The whole place looks like it's coming apart at the seams. The world & me in it. I'm nursing a bottle of Jelinek, set on riding out the night, waiting for all the broken pieces to fall into place, or into a pile. Letting the booze do my thinking for me. It's a bum game.

Maybe if I leave things to drift long enough, they'll look after themselves. After all, nothing's really a mystery, as Regen used to say, except in the way you look at it. It's the seeing that needs solving. Things themselves are just what they are. And what they are is like what a mirror is. A smear of light reflected in glass.

On the squat bandstand in the corner of the room, a stick of a man's hunched over his trumpet blowing a low, plaintive note & holding onto it like a long thread leading through a labyrinth. He's playing to half-a-dozen empty tables. There's a bar by the door. And behind the bar there's a girl with tattoos up & down her arms & a brown bowler hat, gazing at her fingernails. A black Rottweiler lies at the foot of a bar stool, glancing around with large watery dog eyes, being forlorn.

The only other customer is a midget in a ratty antique wedding dress, sipping absinthe & chain-smoking its way through a crumpled pack of cigarettes. Face like a rubber mask. There's a deck of tarot cards spread out on the table in front of it, which it fidgets with from time to time, in that bored mechanical way of someone cheating themselves at solitaire.

Candlelight makes shifting cave-patterns on the walls.

I finger the photograph folded inside my coat & vaguely remember leaving Inessa on a sidewalk somewhere, saying there was someone I needed to meet, or maybe something I had to do, & knowing full well she didn't believe a word of it. But you can't keep looking a confession in the eye. And once I'd made it, telling her about Regen, it was no use. She was just some kid I met in a bar. We'd fucked. I'd let myself pretend she was someone else for a while. I even felt sorry for her, in a drunken nostalgic kind of way. Maybe I'd felt something else too, something I hadn't wanted to feel in too long. But words Blake said once kept coming back. Words that made the drink sour in my mouth. Seeing in my mind's eye his death's-head face leering out of the darkness at me, sleeves rolled up, baring the grey prison scars that covered his arms, saying: "Every confession is a lie."

♠

Things change in ten years, but not everything. The pictures on the banknotes are still the same. Like the faces in the streets. But the denominations don't mean the same things they used to. Time's a veneer that gets sprayed on like that parade of Habsburg kitsch in Old Kafkaville. You dress things up a bit. Change the names. Roll out the new costume drama.

The future looks old already, drained of whatever once made it seem believable. Maybe the hardest thing to learn is that life's meant to be a sham, that species evolve because in the cosmic mind we're just another fiction being told over to keep away the dark.

Only six months ago I was in Paris, sitting in a bar in the Marais, off rue de Rivoli, listening to Blake fill in the missing years. In my head I was still that ghost on the Amazon, staring back at a corpse with ants streaming from its mouth. And then nothing. Scenes skip like faulty playback. A white screen. Needles probing the vein. Insect-brained. Cicadas & fruit bats. Lying awake one morning in a hospital ward in São Paolo & a black nurse talking at me with a red mouth & teeth. Red, black, white. And too many voices to separate into words. Days getting longer & then shorter, until one big sleep, floating out across the vast delta into the capsizing barbiturate sea, for thousands & thousands of blank identical miles.

The jungle became a ward, became a ship, became a city. Somewhere, someone was busy flipping all the switches in the big reality show. Waking from one episode to the next, like you're stuck on the wrong side of the screen looking out, but only seeing what's *on* the screen.

In the ward, some men came to see me. Called me by the dead man's name. Asked lots of questions I didn't understand. They told me a story, about how I'd been found, skin & bones in a canoe out in the Amazon delta, lucky, they said, to be alive. I laughed. It was all I could do. And the more people who came to ask questions, the more I laughed. I felt like a kind of rag-doll Buddha, propped-up on pillows in a hospital bed, laughing at the world's foolishness.

Finally a doctor came & told me I was well enough to go home. I thought that was funny as hell, too. Some goons from an office turned up. They'd've put me on the next plane out of there if I hadn't managed to give them the slip & hitch a ride on a Venezuelan freighter. East to Casablanca, north to Le Havre. The great stench of Europe wafting over the sea.

Everything seemed to happen by itself, as if in reality I had no part in it. Like a game of chance you begin by playing but which ends up playing you. It's always been that way, for as long as I can remember. The world only appears to be coincidence & accidents, but in reality everything's decided, right down to the specifics, even if you'll never know when, or where, or how. You take what's offered, because if you don't it'll drive right over you.

I sometimes think if Regen hadn't appeared that day at the bus stop in Božice I'd still be humping carcasses somewhere or drinking my unemployment cheque, since the town ended up shutting the abattoir anyway. After my mother died, I just got angry & the anger paralysed me. And my old man, the Big Boss, hanging over me – whose very existence was the deciding factor in everything.

If you want the truth, I never really knew my father, I only knew I hated him. What I didn't know then was there are many ways to hate. But hate, like desire, needs to be fed, the way a junky needs to feed his habit. It was Blake who tried to teach me nothing's ever fixed in stone, that everything exists only once, uniquely, that things can be their own cause. The mistake is believing that anything remains the same. A person, a place, an atom, or an idea. *Toujours pour la première fois*. Always for the first time. Familiarity's just an illusion. The way sleep's an illusion. But it's just as easy for a man to be murdered in his sleep as in a jungle full of wild beasts. And I think of those stories Regen used to read to me, out of ancient mythology. Like the one about a man chained to a rock & everyday a vulture comes & tears his liver out, & every

103

night his liver grows back, so that each time the vulture tears it out is really the first time. The first agony. The first fear.

They say the body can't remember pain, but I'm not so sure. You watch a junky going through withdrawal & it always seems like the body's been storing up all that pain in special pain-memory banks just waiting for the day the junk runs out. Hate's different. You can fill yourself up for years with it until it's the only thing you live for & maybe you die of it too. Get a dose too big & too pure it fries your brain right down to a cinder. But you miss the connection & the hate shrivels up like a turd baking in the sun.

Some people are wired for hate, but mostly hate's a discipline you have to work at. Refining it, keeping the corrupting elements out. Synapse eugenics, Blake called it. You've got to keep a pure store against the *day to come*. And the day always does come. Like Christ looking up from the cross & realising for the first time there's no way out.

You lose the faith, *muchacho*, & everything else crumbles away.

♠

The bar I'm in has a name, but I can't remember what it is. Before the Nazis & then the Commies took over, it was supposed to've been a synagogue. All it looks like now from the outside is a bricked-in garage in the courtyard of an apartment building off Šternberkova, full of salvaged junk. Ten years ago, more or less, it was just another post-revolution dive. In those days the regulars were still mostly vagabonds, beggars, drunks, junkies, ex-felons, & plain old certified nut cases. One-time dissidents gone to seed in the few short years since the Wall came down. You kept an eye out for the flying glasses & pissed outside against the wall. From time to time an ape in the corner would pick a fight

104

with himself, hunched-over flailing at the back of his head with closed fists. Maybe ram himself into a doorpost for good measure.

But like so much else nowadays in the Golden City, the place is unrecognisable. You give the barmaid a bowler hat & install a midget by the front door & – *voilà!* – the joint's almost respectable. The only thing missing's a rabbi at the altar & a congregation to *ai-ai-ai* in time with the jazz.

I remember one night, back when Regen & I were still living by the docks, when I'd wandered into this part of town more or less at random, & as usual hard-up for a drink. I strayed in while that crazy poet Magor, all flabby & boozed up to the eyeballs, was throwing his clothes off dancing naked on the tables. His claim to fame was peddling a rock band no-one could bear to listen to anymore. A drunk who'd been leaning against the bar jabbed me with his elbow. Wanted to confide some learnèd opinion of his that this Magor was really just another ex-Bolshevik on the make. Like dancing on a table with a shrivelled dick in your hand was a noteworthy political statement.

"Democracy," the drunk said, slurring his syllables to press his point, a line of spit hanging from his chin, "is just communism's new clothes, see?" I didn't know what the hell he was talking about. When the revolution happened, I was just another dumb kid on a farm in south Moravia. It had nothing to do with me. But maybe the drunk was right. Every pimp I ever met used to be a communist.

Well maybe the past is never as bad as we make it seem. Or maybe it's worse. You grow up in a shithole that could just as well've been paradise itself, now that it's gone.

This is what I'm thinking when the door beside the bar opens & who should walk in but Inessa. She stands there just inside the doorway, eyes searching the gloom. I sink deeper into my chair. On the other side of the room, the stick figure with the trumpet has traded the bandstand for a stool & is siphoning spit from a valve. The drummer slouches behind his miniature drum kit, brushes in hand, like a puppet waiting to have its strings twitched. The accordionist is making silent hand gestures which in the room's chiaroscuro look unreal.

Inessa makes no move away from the door. There's a cold draft coming in, upsetting the midget's arrangement of cards & making the oil lamps sputter. The midget & the three musicians all turn & look at her. She doesn't seem to notice. Finally she stumbles back out into the night. The girl in the bowler hat steps from behind the bar & closes the door. I realise I've been holding my breath the whole time, like a thief in the dark afraid of being caught.

# 16

## SNAKE HOUSE

Eyes. Mouths. Faces cut from old magazines stuck up over sheets of newsprint. Yellowed, pre-revolution, the print illegible. Where the walls had been plastered, the whitewash stood out in dark blotches under dim 40 watt light. Ripped chunks of wall-board lay strewn about the floor. The place was covered in an inch of dust. There were old footprints. Animal tracks. Crumbling wasp nests.

Whatever I'd expected didn't matter. I was already seeing things with a kind of finality. An x-ray vision through layers of time. I'd parked the stolen heap where I figured no-one would see it, if anyone ever happened to come along. We sat there in the dark for an hour, waiting for dawn, the shape of things gradually forming in the gloom. Sunlight broke all of a sudden through black clouds, setting the house & lake aflame. I watched the scenery burn & then fade & a grey light settle over everything like ash.

Regen sat in the car & didn't move. I thought if I waited long enough she'd fall asleep, but she didn't, so I cased the house to make sure it really was deserted the way she'd said it was. And that's when I saw the pictures on the walls, through the boarded-up front window. Something about those cut-up faces spooked me. Lost souls. I wondered who'd taken the time to stick them all up there.

A porch stood out on the side of the house facing the lake & a half-sunken jetty. Wooden palings sloping down into the water. An outhouse tilted against a nearby tree. The porch sagged when I stepped onto it & invisible rats scurried underneath. Spiders gleamed on webs strung between rafters. Wings flapped.

The back door had a rusty padlock that came apart after a couple of blows. Inside was a small laundry. Sagging cardboard boxes stuffed with rags & generations of mouse holes gnawed through. Shelves stacked with empty glass jars, paint tins, cans of marine lacquer, turpentine.

Through the laundry & into the room with magazine faces stuck all over its walls. To one side, a kitchenette with a pair of rusty hotplates, a mouldy fridge & a couple of empty gas canisters. To the other, a doorway led to a smaller room, with a half-collapsed bed frame & mosquito net reeking of DDT.

Whoever owned the place hadn't cared about it in years. Regen always called it the Snake House, something she heard once. But it was no more than a shack. White clapboard turned mostly grey with mould & general decomposition. The lake behind it was half-choked with reeds. Midges hovered everywhere. Eels rippled a surface of black water.

♠

Regen didn't sleep all that day. She sat huddled at the end of the bed, cigarettes burning down between her fingers one after another. I felt lost. When I tried to touch her she flinched. Her eyes were hidden behind the shadows of her hair. I thought if I nodded off, I'd wake up & she wouldn't be there. I walked around the house doing whatever I could to keep my mind awake. I'd never been so tired in my life.

It was late August. Outside the sun was already high above the trees. The clouds had evaporated. A fierce heat radiated from the sky. The air over the lake shimmered. Nothing else seemed to move. I wandered between the rooms like a ghost, not knowing what I was doing there. I'd jerk awake staring at a wall, only inches from my face. A voice kept telling me: "Nothing's ever for free."

I checked on Regen. She hadn't moved. A blackened cigarette butt stuck out between her fingers. I started the routine again, searching for something, not knowing what. Regen looked like she'd cracked. I kept waiting for her to fall asleep. Then it'd be okay. She'd wake up & everything would be the way it used to be. But I was afraid – if I wasn't vigilant enough she'd run away again or, Christ knows, try to kill herself even, the way my mother had. There was no shortage of means: shards of broken glass in the windows, behind the boards that'd been nailed from the outside – coils of rope amongst the junk piled in the kitchenette cupboards – rusted razorblades in the sink – rat bait – turpentine – a meat cleaver wedged deep into a chopping block crusted with eel skin – the lake, with its reeds & cold water. Violence offered itself everywhere I looked.

♠

It was after midday when I realised she was gone. The heat inside was unbearable. A crazy panic overcame me. I charged out among the trees, found the empty car, the empty laneway, choking back my fear. The air buckled & swayed in the heat, the deafening sound of cicadas everywhere. I couldn't think. The sky weighed down on me. I had to struggle to breathe. If I lost her in my mind, I thought, I'd lose her forever. I ran along the dirt laneways, searching everywhere for tracks, footprints, any sort of clue, thinking only irrational thoughts. Hours passed. The heat, unrelenting. Every path led to a dead end.

I walked back to the house to begin all over again. But it was only after I'd stopped looking that I found her – hanging over the back porch, retching into the grass like a sick cat. A white singlet drenched with sweat clung to her back. The rest of her was naked. I stood in the doorway & watched the tremors shake her body, the crust of my father's scum visible between her thighs. I couldn't help picturing the two of them. His coarse hands all over her. His cock sticking in her mouth. Her arse. Her cunt. A glistening slug in the half-light. A sliver of shit. A blood sausage.

I smashed my hand into the doorpost & felt the wall tremble. Blood formed on my knuckles. I smashed again & again. Then something made me stop. I stared at the splinters sticking in my skin. Black & white. I began picking them out when I heard Regen. She'd backed all the way along the porch & was staring at me wide-eyed. I could already see her making a run for it. The white palings of the collapsed jetty gleaming under the water. The hissing of the reeds. Her hair spread out on the rippling surface, bejewelled with dragonflies.

The muscles in my thighs twitched.

"What're you afraid of?" I said. Thinking, you try to lull an animal before you slaughter it, or the meat will taste of fear. Taking a step towards her. The boards straining under the weight. Her hands began creeping up over her breasts, backing herself into the corner of two railings. "It's me," I said, moving closer. "It's okay."

"Don't touch me," her voice paper thin.

"It's okay. No-one's going to hurt you." Another step, & another. And then it was too late. But she didn't run. Instead she flew at me, blindly, like a cornered animal, her fingernails at my face. The fury of it stunned me. I staggered, seeing only red. Then bit by bit I took her fury into me, absorbing it. I used my size to smother her blows. For a long time she struggled, her nails like claws. Teeth. Elbows. Feet. I weathered her violence, crushing her in a slow choke until finally the blows stopped & her body went slack in my arms. The air around us swelled with the low sound of blood beating in my ears. My lungs burned. Everything began going dark.

♠

Regen lay on the dirty mattress with her long hair clinging to her shoulders. She'd dyed it back almost to its natural colour. Late sunlight through the wood criss-crossing the window gave it a tarnished look, like brass. Her head hung to one side, the whites of her eyes visible beneath eyelashes rolled back crazily. If it weren't for her breathing – a sick animal-rasping down in her throat – she might just as well have been dead. Something about her stillness aroused me. I stared at her body. Her dirty feet, her knees drawn up, the stubble around her unwashed vagina, the shape of her breasts through the white singlet. Her wrists were beginning to swell where the rope had chaffed them, tied together to the rope around her neck. Her hands clasped against her right cheek, like a picture of a child asleep.

I told myself it wasn't me. That *thing* in my mind. That other thing, full of anger, making me stuff a half-limp cock inside her. Watching myself, like a shadow on a wall. Seeing instead the image of my father fucking her. And seeing me there fucking him, getting harder, ramming it into him. One blow at a time. Harder & harder until I came. And Regen, her body shuddering beneath me, inert, eyelids twitching. Her singlet transparent with the sweat pouring out of me. I forced myself to kiss her slack mouth, my head swollen with blood, trembling. The taste of vomit on her lips.

For an instant her eyes opened, unseeing. But in them I saw the reflection of my own face & the ugly thing it'd become. In my shame I slapped her & keep slapping her.

111

Fucking & slapping. Groaning as I came again – more painful, eviscerating, deadening.

I rolled off her into a ball, teeth sunk in my knee, eyes knotted. Somewhere in my head I heard her sobbing the way my mother used to sob. A strangulated sound through a half-open door. But it was only the sound of my own sobbing.

♠

That evening the nightmares began. The house by the lake was dark. I crouched outside, among the reeds, watching the full moon begin to rise over the slanted roof. It'd grown cooler. A faint breeze across the water. Inside, Regen lay unconscious, just as I'd left her. I told myself it was for her own good. Let her sleep. Let her know nothing of the night to come. In the morning I'd untie her, wash her body with my own hands, wake her with kisses. We'd be free, purified, now that fate was driving me to do what should've been done all those months ago. Never to have set foot on that train to Prague, but to have sought vengeance then & there, in the full light of day, like a man. But reason gives birth to monsters. Fearful, malformed, unkind beings. I filled my hands with mud from the lake & painted my face with it. An animal emerging from the darkness. A short-haired snout. Yellow tusks glinting in the moonlight.

# 17

## CELLULOID

The night wears on. It's already after midnight – one more midnight in a never-ending chain. The zoots are winding-up their act, accordion sounds warping like fairground nauseas. The old synagogue has taken on that half-demented, two-dimensional cubism things do after you've been awake too long – flattened-out & up-close. The oil lamps glow a dim orange as though someone had tried & failed to snuff them out. I'm fed up with myself, but still not drunk enough to slop out the recriminations. It seems like too much work. I've reached the end of the bottle & about to call it quits when my phone rings. I glop at the handset. There's a number blurring out of it. I hate these things, but it came with the barge job. Every now & then the Greek phones up to make sure no-one's nicked his pile of scrap.

"I'm not here," I say, ignoring the voice at the other end. "Don't leave a message."

"Stay where you are," Blake shouts, loud enough to be heard over the droning accordion. "I'll be there in ten minutes." I stare at the blank screen suspiciously, thinking about all those secret microchips they put in everything nowadays to keep track of you. And how the hell could Blake find me at night in this city anyway? But I give up & let the chair suck me down into a vague, plotless half-sleep, like sinking in water. Concentric circles ripple a surface that's already too far away. My heart thumps out an irregular rhythm. A drum-line spiralling to a dull thud.

♠

I'm walking along a street with someone following me. I can't see who it is. It's night. The street's unfamiliar. It could be anywhere. A city. Orange streetlights. I hear the footsteps of the person tailing me like an echo. I walk faster & the echo pursues me, I slow down & it backs away. I wait around corners, reverse directions, cross & re-cross bridges, underpasses, intersections. But the footsteps are always there.

After walking around like this for what seems an age, I come to a dead end. There's a high chain-link fence cutting the street off from a vacant lot. I struggle not to panic. Behind me my pursuer waits, biding his time. I grab at the wire fence & try to pull myself up, but I can't get a grip. The effort's hopeless. There's no way out.

It's then I notice the coat hanging on a coat hanger that someone's left there on the fence. A brown leather Gestapo coat. It moves slightly, as if something alive were inside it. A dog keens in the distance. The sound of a bottle breaking. A doorway opens & a pair of children sneak out onto the sidewalk carrying a television set between them. On an impulse I make a run for the doorway, but the door's locked. A scurrying of feet. There are no names on the doorbells. No house number over the door. Somewhere above, a window opens. A match flares in the dark. I look up & see a faceless man in a white butcher's apron smoking a cigarette. From behind him, music on an old record player crackles loudly. A metallic orchestra at the wrong speed.

Everything slows down in time to the music.

I shrink away. At my back something makes a noise. I turn around. A man's standing beneath a lamppost on the other side of the street, dressed like a tramp, singing to himself. *Baby face. You've got the cutest little baby face.* Without thinking I start walking towards him. As I come closer, I realise the man's standing in front of a large dressing mirror that's been propped against the lamppost. There are two of him now. One with his back turned & the other facing me. I'm standing in the middle of the street watching him as he applies makeup in the mirror. A face painted like a circus clown's – black crescents for eyes, mouth twisted in a grotesque smile. A face I recognise, turning white in a sudden flare of headlights.

♠

"So we meet again," the voice says, coming from the darkness at me. I open my eyes & there's Blake. It takes time to get him into focus. He's got that faintly manic look he always has when he's on the edge of a come-down. Face constantly shifting around as though it won't stay together in one piece – a head like a Rubik's cube with all the coloured squares sliding off.

I groan. A few more people have come into the bar while I've been asleep. The band's packing up. Ashkenazi jazz whispers from a pair of dusty speakers. Blake sits down across from me & makes his face into a grin.

"Voilà," he says, pulling out a copy of one of the daily scandal rags from his coat. *Plešk*. He spreads it on the table, pushing the empty bottle aside.

I wave him away, yawning. "Yesterday's news."

"There's no news like old news, *muchacho*. It always has a habit of sticking around. What did Marx say? History repeats, first as coincidence, then as inevitability."

"Marx never said that."

"No?"

"Anyway," I groan, "necessity's just coincidence admiring itself in the mirror."

"And I thought you didn't believe in coincidence."

"I don't."

"*Bueno, muchacho*," he says, pointing a yellow finger at the page in front of me. "In which case, this won't interest you at all." He lets the grin slide from his face. "It's the morning edition. Hot off the press. I was just at the news office delivering some prints. I thought you'd want to read it, seeing as how…" His voice trails off without finishing the sentence.

Against my better judgement I look at where he's pointing.

♠

The story's buried on page eight, between two column-widths on Helmut Newton, dead in an LA car crash, & an ad for RUSSIAN LADIES escort agency. It takes some effort to decipher the fundamentals. Some hack had cooked up a tale of woe about what drives young women to suicide. Case in point: unidentified girl drowned at Trója. Body discovered Friday. Suspected suicide. The word *suspected* stands out. No mention of the girl being naked or rope marks around her neck. Something's wrong. It vibes suppressed evidence, undercover investigation. And then the story veers off completely, about the two fishermen who'd pulled the corpse out of the river. Tweedle Dumb & Tweedle Dee. A thumbnail photo of two mugs posing like they'd just landed the catch of the day. I wonder how *Plešk* missed the scoop.

"Someone sold the paper a bum story," I say.

"Maybe there wasn't any story."

"What's that supposed to mean?"

"Means maybe there wasn't any story."

"Sure, & maybe the girl in the newspaper isn't the girl in the morgue, right?"

"Maybe."

"And maybe the girl in the morgue didn't drown herself, either."

116

"Maybe that too."

"Fuck maybe."

In an ideal world all those maybes ought to add up to alternatives. You change the names, the faces, the situations, & everything turns out differently. Lives unlived, roads not taken. As if an alternative's worth a damn unless it's a better one.

Picture a kid in some claphouse down on the border, telling herself all those beautiful lies about how one day she'll make it in the big time in the Golden City. A kid fresh from hicksville with a baby bundled in newspaper left in a dropbox. Desperate calls from phone booths. Selling herself for the price of a coffee & a pack of cigarettes & a one-way ticket to nowhere. There's a crucifix on a silver chain around her neck. She still believes in things. Like redemption, eternal salvation. But none of that matters because whoever she is, she's dead. Dead as a drowned dog.

"I liked the original version better," tossing the paper back at him. "This one stinks."

"You want to see your name in the headlines?"

I can feel the hair bristling along my neck.

"Enough comedy for one day, okay?"

Blake laughs. A dry rasping noise that comes out of his throat. I can't see what's funny.

"Relax, *muchacho*. I'm doing you a favour," he says. "Here," sliding a hand across the table. He plants a neatly folded square of tinfoil in front of me. "It's a gift. No hard feelings."

I look at the square of foil. There's something wrong about it. It resonates some sort of Blake mindfuck. My fingers start tapping on the edge of the table.

"What is it?"

"Look & see."

"You're trying to mess with my head."

117

"On the contrary, my friend. I'm trying to help you clear your conscience."

Without another word, he gets up & crosses the room in a series of fluid movements. There's a suit sitting at the bar who wasn't there before. Blake shoulders him out of the way. The suit tries to make himself look annoyed, but thinks better of it & slouches off. Blake signs to the barmaid in the bowler hat & calls for a bottle. He makes a gesture of snapping a photo of her. She laughs, the tip of her tongue wetting her top lip. Shoves a bottle of brandy across the zinc-top & chalks it up on the tab.

♠

I hold up the square of celluloid against the candlelight. The image is hard to make out at first. Figures in negative, flickering in & out of focus. Like staring into a pool of water that won't stay still. Blake sinks back into the chair opposite, settling a bottle of Jelinek between us. Pours two glasses. I watch him wipe his face with his hands, eyes half-crazy. Pervitin-mad. He looks like a death's head in the jungle. Totem figure. He's forcing me to become part of my own delusions.

I stare back at the crumpled tinfoil lying on the table in front of me. I'm drunk. I don't even know if what I'm seeing is what's really there.

"So," Blake's voice, calling me back. "What'll it be?"

I try to shake the image from my head. Aware there are other people here. Distant underwater voices. A double bass thuds rhythmically. A glint of light from silver foil. Something swimming through the room's chiaroscuro. Scales of a fish glinting in a shaft of sunlight coming from above. A lure on the end of an invisible line. You reach out to grasp hold of it. And then what? Blake yawns. The music ends.

Without saying anything I let the negative dip into the candle's flame & catch light. It flares momentarily then turns to smoke.

"Plenty more where that came from," Blake says, planting his hands on the table. There are scars on each of the knuckles. Grey runic knots of damaged flesh where someone had stubbed out a dozen cigarettes. There were other scars, too. Knife scars. Settling old scores. In La Paz, though, he always carried a gun.

"So what?" I shrug.

Across the room I notice the midget flip another card onto the table. The stereo blares. Parrot-screech of saxophone in sudden crescendo. Blake sighs. He makes a tired face at me, letting his right hand drift across to the glass in front of him. He lifts the glass to his lips & drinks the brandy down slow. Puts the glass back on the table. Unhurried & deliberate.

"Life's a game," he says, "isn't it? Nothing's ever as far beyond comprehension as we pretend it is." His eyes get me into their focus. "When it comes down to it, there's only this – what we're permitted to see, & what we refuse to see. And it happens that from time to time we need someone, or something, to open our eyes for us. The question is, does it matter," he goes on, "if what we see, or what others see, is true or not? When all's said & done, who decides what's true anyway?" Blake fingers the bottle cap as he speaks, turning it & turning it. "You, for example," he says, spinning the cap across the table. It comes to rest against my hand. "You can always chose to believe what you want to believe." That grin again. "But be careful, *muchacho*. What you believe is what you just might get."

Or maybe he says something else. But I've stopped listening. I'm sick of the sound of Blake's voice, of my voice, of everyone's voice. All by itself some demon of intention pokes a finger into my mind's eye. My hands ball into fists. Blake's smiling now. A grotesque circus clown smile. He has my father's eyes. Black holes of mocking ruthlessness. A head stuck on a pole like some god-fetish in the jungle. Supai. Nightmare demon.

"Remember what they say in the classics," he says, in a dried-up toneless voice, rictus-jawed. "Don't fuck a gift horse in the mouth."

# 18
## REALISM

Sometimes I have trouble remembering things the way they happen. Or else I remember too well & reality palls. The sorts of things in my head wouldn't make sense in any photograph. A camera only sees effects, not causes. Like some cold-blooded thing eyeballing you through a pane of glass. It's the photographer's demon who gives the image its psychology. The god in the machine who seduces the way you see. Turns a naked body into pornography. A morgue shot into a pietà. Fiction into real life.

As a rule, Blake only photographed the women he fucked. What he said: "I want to be inside them, to understand them, their fears & desires." His idea of anything's to get in under people's skin, find out what makes them tick, then screw around with the mechanism. There's no such thing as too deep. However far you go, there's always some place deeper.

A couple of weeks ago I was standing outside a gallery on Národní street, pissing in the wind & ogling the passers-by. It was the night they were opening Blake's show. The place was full of black ties & mutton done-up in taffeta, slumming it for thrills. A couple of stooges in waistcoats were rationing out fake champagne & little boiled sausages skewered on toothpicks. Blake cruised up late on his Enfield, then spent the rest of the time slouching in a corner watching the crowd like a spider watches flies.

Whoever dreamt-up the show had the bright idea of calling it *Le Déjeuner Nu*. They'd printed a type of phonesex menu & stuck it outside the entrance on a lightbox. Mugshots with the eyes blacked-out. Asian, Caucasian,

Latino, Negro & everything in-between. Under each mugshot, names like Chloë, Aurore, Christine, Blanche, Isabelle, Claire. Franchise names you can hear any night of the week on Place Pigalle.

The pictures inside the gallery were all large-scale blowups in bloodless textbook anatomical detail. Naked women smoking, lying in bed, looking like they'd just been fucked. Teasers. Sanitised compared to what you'd find in Blake's regular portfolios. The way most art's sanitised. Because even when it's real, it's never real enough.

We were in a cantina in El Alto once when a mob started throwing stones. Some cops beat up a kid & caused a small riot. Without any warning, a couple of plain-clothes began picking-off people in the street with automatic rifles. Bystanders brought an old man into the cantina with his forearm almost shot away. Tendon & bone sticking out. Blood everywhere. A while later the uniforms came & dragged the old guy off, unconscious, to maybe bleed to death in the back of a wagon or get dropped in a ditch somewhere out on the *plano*. I could see in Blake's eyes how it turned him on. The sheer reality of it. The same look when he pointed a camera. Like pointing a gun. *Reality, not realism.* He made pictures the way you make a corpse.

In Bolivia there was a whole industry for that sort of stuff. Snuff magazines right out in the open on news stands beside *El Pais, Correo del Sur, El Diario*. Daily horror shows. Full-page colour spreads of crime scene photographs, autopsies, the whole bag. Even the newspapers were full of it. Gang shootings. Organ thefts. Decapitated prostitutes. Anonymous mass graves. Some sort of death cult at work in the collective unconscious.

But death *per se* didn't interested Blake. He'd say things like: "It's not what the image depicts, its what depicts the image." The same way he talked about women. "A woman," he'd say, "could have any name in the world. You ask her, maybe she tells you something. Chloë, Aurore, Christine. Why not? There are thousands of Chloës, Aurores, Christines. Maybe it's not her *real* name? So what? What *is* a real name? A name you could put a face to? One face in a million?"

A name, in place of some ineffable, unobtainable thing.

"You know, there was a time when people believed that to forget the name of someone who died meant condemning their souls to oblivion. While in some cultures, someone dies & their name dies with them, cut-out of the language the way a tumour is."

The dead girl in the morgue. A face without a name. An image in a photograph. *I only photograph women I fuck.*

♠

Back in real time I'm losing grip on the last little fragments of clarity. Voices swarming around the room. A spiral of noise. I can't recognise where I am. The same place or some other place. Locations mesh in irrational dream-logic. My tongue's thick. Something squeezing it forcefully down my throat each time I swallow. I hold a bottle, end-up, & something wet comes out of it.

The night was going just fine until the picture of the dead girl showed up & then Blake too showed up, like the joker he is. Someone laughs in my ear. There's a whole crowd in here, wherever here is. A couple of tarts are groping a drunk at the bar, feeling for money in his trouser pockets. Fishnets & tight plastic skirts. The walls lurch. I'm sweating. Jungle music comes up out of the floor. Incense. Shapes move in & out of focus. A brunette sitting at the next table is dripping candle wax into a glass. The wax congealing like little foetuses suspended in amniotic fluid.

I look around the room but no Blake. A taste like vertigo under my tongue. The tarts have moved onto their next victim like vultures after carrion. A tramp clutching an empty glass at the bar, mascara running down his face. A shape in a butcher's apron. Ghosts brushing past. Somebody says something. Some rudimentary equation struggling to make itself understood. A square of foil pushed across the table. A match flaring. A piece of celluloid. Déjà vu. Crooked witchdoctor fingers moving through the dark. Faces. A redhead in the morgue. *Maybe she liked it rough. Maybe someone didn't care what she liked.* I feel dirty. Sick. A gap opens on the far side of the room, tunnelling into darkness. The descent beckons. I lunge towards it. The wanderings of Cain. A fringe of leaves. Words not heard before. Beasts these are, of another world.

Light-shift. A door ricochets. I fall through it into an ammoniac stench, face to face with a cracked, shit-smeared lookingglass. Inwardly cast shadows fall across it, obscuring whatever lies within. A man's or a woman's full bloodied mouth. Dark heavy sacks falling from the undersides of eyelids & bulging out over the cheeks. It's an image coagulated with meaningless substance. I see myself & refuse to recognise myself as being that thing.

Laughter. The sound of bees...

A lightbulb flickers. For a moment everything's dark. A frozen retinal darkness. And then the light returns. A mere blink of an eye. A fragment, a ruin, a fiction. Something's alive in there, grunting through a wall. A toilet stall behind a broken wooden door. Mind's eye pornography of two men fucking each other in ways impossible. I push the door open & behind it there's nothing. A hole in the floor. A craggy mouth. I get down on hands & knees to see better what's inside.

Reaching down afraid the way as a boy I was afraid. Arm covered in leeches where tree roots overhung the river. Regen burning them off with match-heads. Death flares. Black turd-like things writhing on the grass. But the hole in the floor is somebody's face. A dirty white wedding dress spread out. Vomit down the front. Echo of something coming from its mouth. The house of cards comes tumbling down. The Drowned One. *Utopenec.* Lying in its own piss.

My hands shake. The hag midget in its wedding dress lies there snoring on the cubicle floor, clutching a tarot deck like it's clutching a bridal bouquet. The hem of its dress has slipped up to reveal the top of a pair of soiled miniature stockings. Perspiration stings my eyes. Blink. Look closer. A hand, mine, reaches out & slowly pushes the hem of the dress higher. Up over the thighs. Nosing the coarse damp black hair curling over wax flesh. Misshapen hips. The straps of a lace garter-belt framing a blood-dark oversized penis where the cunt should've been.

I reel back. A snaking hiss, coiling & striking out from the shadows. The midget in the wedding dress lies there immaculate as a pietà. A naked bulb overhead, flickering.

All of a sudden the room's full of gaps. I'm fearful of being sucked into one of them. Blake's laughter. A parrot screech in the jungle. I see a dead man slip into darkness as a canoe moves away from a river bank. Monkey voices. The river moving faster the further I drift from shore. Rushing now. Rats behind the bulkheads. A ship's horn. Le Havre. A woman with her head wrapped in a pillowcase, screaming.

I beat my head against the wall until the demons go quiet. A wave of calm. The shit-smeared mirror drips with sarcasm. *You'll look the part at least.* I heave into the sink. A bouquet of brandy & slime. Brown water gushes from a tap. My hands do things to my face. I try to focus on one thing at a time. Feet on the floor. The face in the mirror almost familiar now. Like a face in negative. A face that doesn't belong there.

# 19
## WIND BECOMES WATER

You get up from a chair & begin falling,
& the falling doesn't stop.
                    Sound of a wet finger circling the rim of a glass.
                        It's cold. The ghost of someone.
        A flame touching the tip of a cigarette.
                    Somewhere, a room, a box on an ocean.
Not because you're afraid that you won't wake up, but because
of what you're afraid you'll...
                        Another drink & then another.
            "Look into my eyes."
    Two faces joined in a maze of smoke & candle lights.
                                    A laughing
                                        cunt.
                    Valves like a saxophone's.
        Shadows. Something naked in a mirror.
                            *Knuper, knuper, kneischen.*
Blake walks in from outside the room, outside the frame.
        Totem-faced.
                    Shrunken head on a pole.
                                Matted rat-
                                    hair.
            A flame touching the tip of a cigarette.
                You fuck & you pay, *muchacho.*
A cold coin pressed to the nape of your neck.
                            Another drink & then.
            Mouth a Rorschach blot.
Saying not because I'm afraid.
            Faces moving around a room to the darkest places.

127

Sound of a wet finger.
Eyes rimmed with sodden lashes.
Rain at the window. Spiralling.
Mid-get. Mid-get. Mid-get. Mid-get. Mid-get. Mid-get.
Blake walks in.
The dead girl, her mouth next to your ear.
Do you want to find me? Or be free of me?
Rain.
Her mouth.
*Der Wind, der Wind. Das himmlische Kind.*

♠

When you cover your ears, the wind becomes water. Time slips back into shadows. Sunlight. The barley in the fields. Black grapes weighing on the vines. A bird sits on a wire fence, cocking its head to one side. Listens. Comes closer along the wire, awakened to curiosity.

I lie there, watching the clouds merge & separate. A hundred thousand mental images all taking shape in the one space. The sound of water becomes the sound of bees. I try to concentrate. With no-one else around, it's easier. The sky slips on its reel like a piece of celluloid. The image jags. Something dark crosses my field of vision. Black plumage on grey. Jackdaw. I see the bird peering at me. An expressive eye. It opens its beak & leans forward. I realise it's speaking to me, but I can't make out what it's saying.

♠

The scene begins again. I see myself, like a spectator watching at a distance. Lying there like an infant in a cradle. I think of a nursery rhyme. Wind rocking the shadows, back & forth like water. The sky is an ocean, as vast as time. A great big

128

blue sphere whose edges are invisible. It wraps around the eye, waiting to swallow it. I think of somebody falling. A hole in space & a man falling through it, born into the void.

Somewhere a muted ethereal horn sound. A hanging note. Silence. Then a whole cascade of notes spilling out of the sky like some crazy jazz. Reeling, suffocating, searing. A man in a bathtub in the middle of a sea, hair blown back, clinging to the shower-pipe like a boatswain clinging to a ship's mast. The crazy music swirls. The sea like a warped lens. And that voice again, echoing through the jazz. I shut my eyes. The storm of noise sweeps over me in waves, wave after wave. Everything heaves.

♠

I open my eyes. The wind's still now. I'm standing with my bare feet on the earth, in the grey soil. Black trouser legs against pale feet. The sky glows above the vineyards, a virgin azure. A jackdaw's roosting on the head of the shower pipe, hanging over the old bathtubboat. Gurgling craw-sounds, words lost in transmission. It tilts its black head, a black eye beadily gazing down. I follow its gaze.

A young girl's lying at my feet, pale hands tied together, a loose cord around her neck. Her hair's been brushed down on either side of her face, garlanded with white lilies, a pall of white silk veiling her body. She's beautiful, even though she's dead. What would her name have sounded like? The jackdaw flaps its wings, shifts on its perch. Two women in black stand at the foot of the corpse, turning rosaries in their hands.

Without thinking I kneel down beside the young girl's corpse, brushing my fingers along the side of her face. Touching her hair, her mouth. She lies there with her eyes open, staring through me. I look & look but no reflection appears in them. Only a green-grey film of trapped light.

129

I plunge my hands into the earth & begin burying her. One handful of earth at a time. The grey soil spills across her face, her livid mouth, her eyes. Across the white silk veiling her breasts, her sex. Sifting through her hair. A grey halo of dust hangs in the air.

I hear the two women mutter as I work, turning their rosaries between their fingers. *Ave Maria, gratia plena*. The jackdaw gurgles, a priest intoning. *Requies…* I work & work, hands blackening, earth spilling over the edges of the cracked enamel tub. I work like a man erecting something. Imbued with purpose. A mound of earth with a rusted pipe standing up out of it.

♠

It's grown dark. But even in the darkness the grave's clearly visible. I look around but the two women are gone. The jackdaw rustles its greyblack plumage. The smell of turned soil suffuses everything. Somewhere, in a distance I can't even begin to fathom, a note rings out & fades. A bell. A small bell like a bell on a child's bicycle. It rings again, closer this time. I turn around in the dark trying to locate the sound. But the sound moves as I move.

I see a light approaching through the vines. Weird silhouettes bending & looming. I follow the direction of the light out onto a dirt road. There's the stone wall & the gate. And behind it, the old farmhouse with its windows lit with a blue TV aquarium flicker. In front of the gate, a very small man in a white bridegroom's suite is riding a bicycle around in circles. He rides slowly & seems at any moment about to lose his balance. With each completed circuit he rings the bell on the handlebars, a round headlamp tracing erratic patterns on the ground.

For a long time I stand on the edge of the dirt road & watch the tiny man in the white suit peddling his bicycle. Curious, perhaps, to see if he'll fall off. But each time he appears on the verge of losing his balance, he somehow rights himself, & turns again.

♠

It's the turning that reminds me of the teacher drawing circles within circles on a blackboard in coloured chalk. An orange circle for Mercury. A blue circle for Venus. A green circle for Earth. A red circle for Mars. And in the middle, a large orange disc for the sun. And I wondered why the sun didn't have a name the way the planets did & the other stars did. Sirius. Alpha Centauri. Betelgeuse. And if it was because people used to call the sun God, which was silly, because the teacher said the sun was made of gas, like hydrogen & helium. And when the sun finished burning all the gas, it'd turn brown & fade & everything on Earth would die. Which was like Revelation, except that in Revelation God didn't turn into a cold brown thing in outer space. A cold brown dwarf thing & not a black hole. And I thought how the idea of a black hole really would be like the idea of God. And that maybe God was whatever was on the other side.

♠

On the other side of the farmhouse gate, the stone wall runs along a yard where it joins an old barn with brick walls painted white. The barn doors are open. A metal hook hangs from a cross beam, glinting in the moonlight. I hear a sudden beating of wings, a dark shape. The jackdaw's silhouette perches on the apex of the barn roof. Caw-cawing. I realise that the man in the white suit has stopped riding around in

131

circles & is nowhere in sight. At first I feel confusion. Then disappointment. Betrayal.

I cross the roadway. A red bicycle lies on its side in front of the gate. Short white tassels hang from the ends of the handlebars. I reach down & finger the bell without ringing it. It feels warm, like a body. It's a vaguely repulsive feeling. While I'm thinking this a voice comes from the farmhouse. I straighten up & stare at the flickering blue square of light where the window should be. Then the front door opens. The little bridegroom is standing in the doorway, beckoning at me to follow him inside.

♠

Inside, the farmhouse is cluttered with bric-a-brac of all descriptions. A cuckoo clock over the mantle groans, its springs coming slowly unwound. Footsteps echo down the hall. I follow. The carpet there is deeper. I turn to the left & then to the right & then left again. The hallway turns in upon itself, at each turn the carpet growing deeper, until it's like wading through undergrowth.

Suddenly, just as I'm about to turn back, the hallway ends. The walls are damp. Humid. Perspiring. A skein of flesh. I feel there's no alternative but to find a way through. My hands grope blindly. Somewhere, on the other side of the wall, there's a voice singing. And then, all by itself, a door opens & light floods out. I find myself in a large white room. Light radiates from no visible source. In the middle of the room, a broken train set lies on the floor. A red toy engine is turning around in circles, on its side like a beetle with a broken back. *Clack, clack, clack.* Against the far wall is a bed beneath a window draped with gauze curtains. A mobile hangs above the bed, with white plastic discs depicting each of the nine planets in orbit around the sun. And there, at the foot of the bed, sits a ventriloquist's dummy dressed in a white suit, its mouth drooping open.

The sound of singing continues.

When I walk to the window & peer out through the blinds, the singing stops. On the other side of the window it's just possible to discern another room. Everything in this other room is also white. I cup my hands to the glass in order to see more clearly. As I gaze around the edges, I realise that this other room is almost identical to the one I'm standing in – except that in the centre of the room, or in the centre of the window, there's a blurred shape which obstructs my view.

I press closer. The blur becomes an outline. I strain to see clearly what it is. And there, looking back at me, from the depths of my own reflection, is a young girl. Her forehead, like mine, pressed to the glass. In her eyes, I can see very clearly the room in which I'm standing. Only I'm not there.

# 20
## MANDALA

I'm nobody. I don't exist. In a night stuffed full of holes, it could be anywhere, any time. The mind in its body, in its purgatory, awaiting absolution. I ought to be dead by now, but I'm not. I'm not *even* dead. There's no excuse. Going on like this. What am I doing? What am I doing *here*? What was I *ever* doing here?

♠

Hunched against the bar struggling not to vomit. On the other side of it, a large mirror swarms in a convergence of reflections. It isn't the same place as before. Blake's gone. Vanished into the night. Took my soul in contract. The demon you own & the demon who owns you. Mumbling into my drink. A name. Nothing more than a name. Like Blake says: *Pas un nom juste, juste un nom* (talking French 'cause it comes-on more profound). And the rain still falling, in the dark, somewhere, far off. In a place perhaps imaginary. *That other girl. The one you lost. The one you always say you're looking for.*

My eyes swim in the deep unfocused background, all shadow & sleight of hand. I've got to get out of here, but I'm not going anywhere. *You came back. What for?* My conscience is clear. *Your conscience is as precious as a fleur-de-lis in a beggar's arsehole.* Blake's laughter. Like the cat in the cartoon that gets the canary. A sound of flapping wings. Someone always gets to laugh last. Just before the end. The gut-laugh of the great almighty. Bye-bye.

But if this is the end, what the hell am I still doing here? And who the fuck am I anyway? A wrong name in a passport, waiting to expire. The name of a town I was never born in. Who is there that knows me? Ha-ha. My head aches. I can't think anymore. A mask in that mirror, multiplying. Like an autism. Head-staggered. Eyes & mouths overlap. A thousand identikit faces.

A character walks out of one story into another, like a ghost. The places all familiar, but the names are wrong. The face in the mirror isn't yours. The one you're looking for doesn't know you.

*Regen.*

Two syllables that barely form. I can't get them out. It's all too late. Salt in my mouth. Red in my eyes. A drunk holding on for dear life. All around the tide's swelling. Inch by inch. But I can't give up yet. I've got to make it to the bitter end.

One more for good measure. Won't feel a thing. Ha-ha. But it's no good, the glass weighs a tonne. It's my anchor. My still-point.

The sea closing in. Blake's voice again. A waxwork's hiss.

I shut my eyes. No use. He's waiting there for me. Sitting at a table, dealing cards. He's laughing. The cards fall faster & faster. A blur of hands. The edges of the cards flutter against a draft that comes from nowhere & everywhere. The room shudders. Cards fall in a shapeless mess. All but one.

And then.

Everything jags back into focus. Blake holds the last card out to me. A pattern in black & white. An ace. The ace of spades.

He turns the card over. On the other side there's…

A face.

A face I recognise. Because it used to be mine.

The room telescopes into it.

135

Flickering.
Like an image in an old film. The centre
of a spiralling
mandala.
That face. Sucking everything in. Vertigo. And
just as I'm about to gag, the film
unravels,
spills from its reel.
Frames of dark light dissolve into one another, erupting
into white sores.
Rancid stench of burning celluloid.
Its taste in my throat. Laughter in my ears.

♠

Meanwhile, or much later – who knows when exactly – I
realise Inessa's standing beside me. Faint neon catches in her
hair, falls across her face. There's a look of sadness about her.
I could ask her what's wrong but I don't. When she speaks,
her words sound like a voice played backwards. It takes a
while to make sense of it. She doesn't seem real. Nothing
does. I try to focus. To see if it isn't just another one of
Blake's demons sent to screw with my mind.

"What're you doing here?"

"I've been looking for you," she says. As though I should
care.

"Hell've I done to deserve that?"

"You should stop feeling sorry for yourself," she says,
taking my glass away & pouring what's left on the counter.
The barman growls something from the other end of the bar.

"You're a tough nut, kid."

"More than you know," she says. "Now stand up."

"I don't wanna stand up. I'm right where I belong."

"Shut up," she says, pulling me off my chair. I grab hold of the bar. But I'm too exhausted to put up a fight. I feel like I've been running an obstacle course set up by unknown opponents. It's a familiar feeling & I know how it always ends. Face down.

But I'm still standing. Inessa has my arm in a grip that's too strong for a little girl like her, but I'm not arguing. My eyes move hazily around the room. A dark room full of white bees. Black bees on white snow. TV static. A row of slot machines blocks off one end of the bar. A couple of shapes mechanically slot coins to make the numbers go around & the lights flash.

I don't have a clue where I am but I feel like I've been here before. That I've always been here before. A room, a nowhere situation, what you might call a predicament. The type of place a man could die in & no-one would notice the difference.

♠

When Blake left me behind in La Paz, it was like he was discarding one of his whores. There's a danger in letting yourself get attached to things. I should've learnt that lesson years ago. I look at this girl who's standing next to me, keeping me from falling down, & wonder what crazy idea she has coming after me. She ought to know that some people are just too ugly to play at redemption. Besides, there's no such thing as a better world. The world's just as ugly & stupid as the people in it & always will be.

Blake was right about that. And maybe he was right, too, that to see what's true in the world you need to make it just a little bit uglier. Like the saints in the Bible communing with filth or offering themselves up to martyrdom. But somehow the lesson was lost. The filth & martyrdom got prettified into art. Christ on the cross. Gratifying humanity's wish for an eternal scapegoat. It made me think of my mother & her strangulated piety. "People always venerate the wrong things," Blake said. "Suffering's everywhere. The crucifixion's beautiful *because it's ordinary*." Well amen to that.

Standing outside the gallery on Národní the night of Blake's opening: "Art," he said, gesturing through the window at the frocks & bowties on the other side, "is civilisation's whore." Sure. A slut dolled-up like a virgin. The oldest hustle in town. "La beauté," he mocked, "sera *banale* ou ne sera pas."

♠

For a long time I'd fooled myself into believing that Blake was a kind of father to me. (Beware of fathers!) When he'd left me in La Paz, I was too sick to think straight. I imagined all crazy things. Seeing Blake everywhere like a voodoo spirit. An evil genius guiding me through the inner night. I don't know how long I stayed there with the fever working its way through me. Time's whatever you believe it is. Just like the truth's whatever you say it is, unless someone can prove otherwise.

I imagined Blake's whores plotting to do me in, while I lay there helpless. Some sort of revenge. Maybe they enjoyed watching me suffer. Maybe they didn't care. I dreamed of the men with machetes. I pictured Blake having his face carved up or getting a bullet in him, out on the altiplano. When I woke from the fever, the boy was there. I'd never seen the kid before. But something about him was familiar. A strange silent boy with Blake's eyes. Witchdoctor's apprentice. Leading me far into the north. From there to make the long journey of purification, ha-ha. Sensing all the while that Blake himself was somehow watching me. Those eyes. A ghost leading a corpse through purgatory.

♠

Back in the here & now, I'm staring at the mirror behind the bar through a gap in the fog. The mask of a lunatic ready to howl at the moon. Inessa's still beside me. She's not an hallucination after all. I try to say something that'll make her reconsider, but I don't even have the energy to be ugly anymore. I tell myself that's okay. There's always tomorrow.

Inessa tosses some money at the barman. He scoops it into the till with a fat, oversized paw & says not to bother coming back. I'd like to vomit in his face, but Inessa's already dragging me towards the door. I gag & stay upright. It seems funny to be walking out on my own two feet, but the show's not over yet.

"Where're we going?"

"Why did you leave me before?"

"Shit. Nothing personal, kid."

"Of course it's fucking personal."

"Ježíš Marjá!"

"Look at you. Big man. You're pathetic."

"I've seen worse."

"Idiot."

"I like you too, kid."

"Idiot."

# 21
## MONKEY'S MOON

No homecoming but a return. A street in a town. Blue squares of windows. The flicker of TV light throwing stark shadows against the walls. How long had I been away? Months or years? Time like some remote, foreign place. As if returning from a truly immense journey, everything I'd once known made strange. The full moon above the telephone lines. Branches shifting in the wind.

A tin can rattled along the street. Cats upsetting the trash in a trash bin. I listened from a distance, becoming one with the shadows. At the end of the street, a rusted metal gate with a NO ENTRY sign turned yellow in the lamplight. Somewhere the sound of water running. Valves of a saxophone. TV dialogue wafting through the trees.

I kept to the shadows, past the NO ENTRY sign, through the vacant lot. A pear tree stood out of the gloom. Long grass, piles of rubble, cracked bricks, corrugated iron. Useless implements jumbled together. A wooden fence cut the yard from the house beyond. The house of my father's father. I picked my way across. I pushed my hands against the wooden fence, ants streaming through split palings, & felt it sway. Something groaned & cracked. A faint light through barred ground-floor windows.

I froze & waited, watching for signs. For the lights to go out. For the old man to turn-in. I clutched at the package inside my coat. A meat cleaver wrapped in a dirty cloth, the wood of the handle smooth in my hand. Time passed. I edged along the fence until I found the gap that'd always been there & slipped through.

I skirted the small concreted yard, avoiding the bins. Silence. In the moonlight, the concrete glistened wetly. The smell of blood & raw meat. A spiral of foamy water around a clotted grate. I breathed deep, filling my lungs. The faint smell of the slaughter yards. A smell you never get away from.

Behind the far wall was the cool-room, discoloured squares of brick & mortar where basement windows used to be. At my shoulder, a pane of dirty glass & grey prison bars. Inside, the room was empty, lit from the stairway through an open door. A row of chopping tables. Knives, saws, mincing machines. A green rubber hose coiled on the floor. Mops & brooms. Black plastic bags, tied & stacked against the wall.

I settled back into the shadows & waited. Felt in my pockets for the house keys. It was only a matter of time now. For the hour to strike. Hands, feet, shadows. An animal in the night, hunting its prey. A curious detachment came over me, aware of this animal within. Mind & instinct. The one that bears witness, & the one that hunts & kills. Over & over I'd calculated the moves until every thought was like a trance. Hypnotised by inevitability. I listened to the noise in my head fading out. Then an upstairs window opened & he appeared. Standing there, smoking a cigarette, face & white apron lit by the full moon. I sensed his eyes move through the shadows, unconsciously seeking me. I sank down silently. I watched. I waited. All reflex now. There was no way out.

♠

What would my mother have thought, to have seen me like that? The full moon up there in the black sky like a cut-out hung on a mobile. The big green, blue & red planets & moons turning on their invisible threads of fishing line. When I was young. Impossibly young. A star chart & a model telescope. To see God with. Dreaming of life on other

141

worlds. Their Roman & Greek names: Mars, Neptune, Pluto, Io, Europa, Titan. Watching the solar eclipse through a hole in a piece of cardboard, facing away from the sun. One day finding a piece of blackened celluloid & staring through it at the strange white orb the sun was behind its fire. A white hole burned into my eye, becoming its opposite. A black dot on a white wall. That grew larger & larger, until it swallowed everything.

It's funny the things you remember. And the things you don't. If I force myself, I can almost picture my father's hand reaching down through the darkening water to grasp hold of me once upon a time, to save me from drowning. First memory. The river behind our farmhouse. The yellow-brown water & his hand. Fingers spread out & rays of light fanning between them. Did he resent having to save me?

Regen & I used to swim there, in that river, for years until my mother died & ruined everything. People would come & trap eels. Often there'd be a bucket of eels sitting in the laundry, stinking the place up. On Sundays my mother would sometimes make dumplings with the blueberries we picked. Our hands & arms, mouths, stained with juice.

Until my mother died I hardly knew my father. He was always somewhere else, doing overtime, returning at night. On weekends he stayed in his workshop. My mother did most of the work in the orchard, pruning the trees while I collected branches & made them into piles at the bottom of the yard. Once a year we smoked the hives & made honey, slicing the waxy honeycomb into cubes to eat.

Whenever my father was around, I'd stay outside. He always mocked the way my mother did things, telling her in so many words she was an idiot. If he was drunk he'd sometimes make a grab for me & give me a hiding for anything at all. I could hear him at my mother from behind their door. It could go on for hours. I'd run out into the vineyards & hide, waiting for something to break.

After the revolution my father's family had the house in town with the old butcher's shop restituted. It happened just before my mother hanged herself. After, when they were packing up the farm, I found a portrait of the communist Gustáv Husák in the attic covered in pigeon shit. I knew who he was from school. My father burnt everything that'd belonged to my mother in a bonfire in the middle of the farmyard. Dresses, shoes, a wedding gown in a box. Even the wooden crucifix that'd always hung on the kitchen wall. Fire gleaming in his eyes.

♠

Someone said once, you return home to go mad. The demons of childhood lying in wait for you.

Inside the house it was quiet. Moonlight played over the walls & floors. Each room opening into another like boxes in a Chinese puzzle. In the middle of the puzzle there'd be the last room, the one in which the mechanism of some diabolical machine would be meshing & spinning crazily like the mind of God.

The staircase groaned beneath my weight. At each step I pressed myself to the wall, holding my breath. No-one stirred. My grandfather slept at the far end of the hall, above the shop front, with his door locked & a cork in each hand – to stave off rheumatism. My father's room was at the head of the stairs. His door was unlocked. I pictured him in bed asleep, lying on his back, mouth open. I listened for the sound of his breathing, suspecting a trap.

Was it really him I'd seen at the window? Was it really him in the apartment above *St Pauli*? Or were there two of him? More even? Demons sent to trick or torment me. I climbed the stairway inch by inch. I concentrated on the door ahead of me. Willed myself towards it. A faint sound of snoring from within. Moonlight burnishing the handle. I watched my shadow pass ahead of me. Reach out. Turn it.

Beyond was a hot, airless place. Stinking of sweat & booze. I stood in the doorway watching. My shadow moved without me. Silently it strode to the head of the bed. Raised its hand. The long rectangular silhouette of the cleaver, lifted high, & for a moment seeming to hesitate. And exactly at that moment, my father's eyes opened. He was staring up at the blade dumbly, a confused expression forming on his face. He couldn't see me, because he didn't believe I was there.

# 22
## ACCORDION

Out of the bar, slosh. A street somewhere. Rain coming down
in fine slanting lines. Apartment buildings at wrong angles.
We walk & walk. Skeleton trees trace shapes in the wind.
Invisible things fluttering in the air. Wet tarmac &
streetlights, scattered across the night like angel dust.
Nothing happens for a thousand miles. Past the art academy.
The park gates. Down the steep embankment & across the
railway tracks.

Inessa has a hand under my arm, leading me I don't know
where. We stop & listen, waiting for a train to materialise
from the dark. But none do. The cold rain gradually sobers
me. Breathing the wet earth. Sap in the trees. The season's
breaking up, mad like all the rest of us. Stirring dull roots.
Reflex & hypothalamus. The brain of winter thawing in its
jar.

The rain turns to drizzle again. Inessa leads me down
along winding paths beneath the leafless canopy. Faint
lamplight reflecting on a darkening sea. The park spreads out
beneath the sky – we dissolve into it, becoming smaller &
smaller. Footsteps echoing. The darkness groaning.

At some point we reach a crossroads. An orange sign
starting out of the gloom points left saying ZOO. We follow
it. I picture wild beasts in cages, stalking back & forth in the
mist. Elephants. Flamingos. Howler monkeys. Giant iguanas.
A whole menagerie. As we walk, Inessa combs her wet hair
with her fingernails, gathering it at the back of her head &
letting it fall loose again. Her other hand's still under my arm
but it's just there & not holding me up anymore. Thinking

how small she is & the burden I'd make for her. Though some people get upended if they don't have a burden to carry around like ballast.

I'm thinking some such idiot thing when I realise Inessa's stopped somewhere behind me. I turn around & she's staring off through a clearing at the edge of the path. On the other side of it, barely visible in the dark, there's an old boarded-up planetarium – a crumbling domed structure nested within the overarching trees. In front of the planetarium there's a small antique carousel, with painted lions & unicorns & horses with tangled manes. A grey tarpaulin hangs over one side. It takes a while to realise where we are.

In the drizzle the painted animals have a strangely mournful air about them. The scene belongs to one of those scaled replicas, a miniature Potemkin village under a plastic dome filled with water & tinsel, that snows when you turn it upside-down. The sort of place you find in fairytales, stumbling lost through a forest.

Inessa whispers something in my ear & slips away among the shadows. Footsteps lost in the gloom. A moment later the lights of the carousel flicker & come on. Cracked gilt mirrors & rusting candy-striped poles shine in the wet. Then the lions & unicorns & horses start going around. Accordion music at half-speed belches from a megaphone, sounding weirdly in the big empty night.

♠

When I was very young my mother took me to see the Berousek circus in Mikulov. A big red & yellow striped tent in a field. We sat in the dark with our scarves around our necks near a coal stove. There was a ring master with high black boots, a top hat & moustache. A woman in a sequined leotard swung on a trapeze. The bears danced. A pair of

146

monkeys ran around doing tricks – one in a little white suit, the other in a tiny white dress. One rode a bicycle, the other rode on the back of a pony & jumped through hoops.

Afterwards we ate ice cream at a stand, even though it was winter.

Carousel music played from a cracked megaphone.

Across a warp in time, Inessa is waving at me. Her hand a pale blur. I watch her go around on the carousel, riding a white unicorn in her black boots. I walk out of the shadows into a pool of light. Climb up beside her on the carousel. Her eyes gleam.

"How'd you do that?" My own voice sounds far away.

"Magic," she says.

As we kiss, water runs down the back of my neck. I feel Inessa's hands on my face. Her tongue in my mouth. The darkened world turns around us to the noise of that cracked accordion music. Around & around like something in a dream. Until the music slows down again & stops. And the fuses blow in a shower of blue starlight streaking the air.

We wait in the dark, listening to the sounds come back from the trees. Wet leaves dripping on the ground. Drizzle turning to mist. We kiss again, slowly. A kiss that begins with the mouth & spreads out through the body – her mouth sweeter than sour plums. She pushes my coat down from my shoulders. Pulls me onto the back of the wooden unicorn, until I'm astride it, with her astride me, our mouths never separating.

It was a kiss that seemed to go on forever. A kiss like the kisses of childhood, full of timeless, unknown things. And when it ended something inside me felt sad. Like the child who was supposed to be me, sitting beside my mother under the big top, watching the bears doing their tired melancholy

147

dance. The grey-haired ringmaster stooping with outstretched hand, coaxing them to one more trick.

How had I become what I am? Looking up at my mother's astonished face, when the trapeze artist somersaulted high in the air. And never suspecting her astonishment was solely for my sake. Holding my little mittened hand. And when it was all over, kissing me on the forehead. And if she hadn't hung herself in a tree, none of this would've happened? And I wouldn't be here now, on a broken carousel, in the dark, in the middle of the night, in the arms of a stranger?

A whisper in my ear says *shhh* & I realise I'm sobbing. Inessa's warm mouth grazes my face. I close my eyes, feel her hand loosen my belt, cold fingers slipping down around my cock. The air surges. My throat tightening. Inessa hushes me. Fingers gently stroking. With a strange tenderness she draws my erection out between her thighs. The encircling cold. And then her warmth enclosing me.

This time we make it slow. A slow rocking like a boat rocking on water. I see myself somewhere far away, in a canoe on a river. It's neither day nor night. It's neither one place nor any other place. I look over the side of the boat & there's Regen lying there, the brown water thick in her hair like honey. Honey running down her breasts. Between her thighs. All of a sudden the air's swarming with bees. Thousands of them. The queen bee & her drones. And I feel their stings suddenly all over me, blinding, convulsing me.

I gasp for breath. Inessa's face hovers in the dark close to mine. Jaw clenched. Her body shudders long & hard as she comes. Silently she clings to me, her thighs tight around my waist. Our breath hangs in the air. We stay that way until the cold makes us ache.

♠

In silence we return to the road through the park. Inessa walks slightly ahead of me, so that I can't see her face. Beneath the overarching trees the road makes a tunnel through the darkness. Water glistening on tarmac. After a long time we reach a fork. Inessa goes on without stopping, taking the turn to the right. The road narrows into an underpass. On the far side of it, a small bridge spans a canal onto an island. We pass stables & an arena. The smell of horse manure hangs in the air. Dogs bark. Unseen birds flap in the trees.

The island's wide. As we cross it, the air seems to grow warmer. In the distance the sky's gradually lightening behind the silhouettes of communist tower blocks, etching-out the hillsides. On the river-side of the island, the air turns sour from the smell of coal smoke. A swaying footbridge runs across to the old Trója palace. Its walls marked by the last flood. And behind the palace, the zoological gardens, echoing with bird-sounds.

Crossing the footbridge I notice the swans asleep on a small outcrop, their plumage stained with the river's filth. The yellow of the streetlights slithers across the face of the water. Nearby a radio starts playing. Voices from a window. A grating of strings. Then a breeze blows up & the music sputters & flaps about & comes wafting back over me. An old cygnet lifts its head briefly & nestles back down into sleep. Inessa stops at the far end of the footbridge, waiting for me. But there's something pricking in my side like a thorn.

I reach inside my undertaker's suit jacket & touch the photograph of the dead girl, sticking out of the pocket. A face without a name. I look away along the river. Breathe its scent, like some primordial maternal scent. My mother, leaning over me in my bed. A lifetime ago. Whispering. A voice, a nursery

149

rhyme. To soothe a child's conscience with. Her scent or my wish-fulfilment of it, too many years old.

This floating little world is all irreversible actions – stepping across a precipice, numb to the fall. But whatever it was, it's too late now. I take the crumpled photograph that Blake had given me & hold it in my hands. It looks like nothing. A piece of paper. I strain to picture the face on the other side of it & whoever it once belonged to. A face in the rain. A girl who'd been a child once, too, trying to find her way in a world where everything loved translates an injustice or tries to be a weapon.

I let the photograph of the dead girl fall into the river. It floats there briefly like a ghost & then it's gone. I turn back towards Inessa. She's standing on the embankment watching me. Behind her a street leads away from the shore, past factories & derelict tenements with graffitied walls & smashed windows. The ruins of a city that's only ever existed in the past tense.

# 23
## CAMERA EYE

The man staring up at me through the blood in his eyes is my father. Time by the clock: thirteen minutes past four exactly. It was a small room, the window lit by streetlights, the walls spattered with cast-back from the cleaver I was hacking him with. One blow after another. But he wouldn't die, he just kept staring at me.

"You're killing me," he said, a statement of fact. Writhing across his bed. My shadow, moving after him – two figures in a savage dance. The room spilled open in a blur. A shadow raising its fist & beating down, cleaver & meat. "You're killing me," he repeated, hooking an arm around my neck, stifling the next blow. Faces pressed close. Forehead to forehead. Breathing hard. We clenched for what seemed like hours, barely moving. The smell of blood on him & reek of stale booze. Red digits of an alarm clock flashed the time in the dark.

I only wanted it to end. For him to lie still & death to come quickly. I felt, as our faces touched, a strange & hopeless tenderness. Like the tenderness you feel for dead things. I thought of my mother's hair. Long & jet black, which I used to breathe-in longingly while she sat & brushed it. The perfume of her stockings. The scent of her underwear in the bottom drawer of the dressing table. Like dead butterflies.

I clasped my father in my arms, telling myself it would be over soon. There was only time left. Blood soaked the sheets of the bed, draining out of him like spoiled wine. They'd hang his carcass above the door for it to whiten. Roast it when the harvest was done. But then he got away. Escaped from me, backwards through the bedroom window, the windowpane exploding into the night.

It happened in the blink of an eye. Slipping from my grip, half tangled in the curtain's white gauze. The sound of glass shattering across the pavement. A fierce wind rushed up from the street. My mind froze. And then I was falling after him, my body acting of its own accord, down into the tunnel of night, the vortex of the streetlamps, a camera eye hurled through space.

♠

They say you've got to be delusional to kill your own father, whereas to kill a complete stranger you only need to realise it's possible. "Blood," my father used to say when it suited him, "is thicker than water." And sweeter, too, when you can taste it. He didn't bleed a single tear when my mother died. It made him angry, though, that she'd cheated him of her suffering. But her suicide was like a black hole in the middle of my existence. And then Regen. And now this.

At the end, I was standing beneath an orange streetlight & he was lying on the bloodied cobblestones, staring up at me the way babies do. I couldn't even tell if he was surprised, or angry, or afraid, or if he was laughing. Making ha-ha sounds like a wounded crow. He had no mouth anymore. Without it, he looked absurd, as if his prick had been cut off. Only the eyes were left. Eyes full of blood.

I could barely lift the blade in my hand. The cleaver had turned to lead. One more blow would've finished him. I pressed the blade against my cheek, wet & cool. But there was nothing left in me. My head swam. If only I could've lain down there beside him, the way I'd lain so often beside

Regen. Father & son. Floating on a sea of red wine. In that old bathtub among the vines. Sailing into the night.

Instead there were voices. Lights coming on. Something called me out of my trance & I suddenly saw myself, standing there, holding a meat cleaver covered with blood in my bloodied right hand. My father's blood. Sangre de Dios. *In nomine Patris, et filii...*

Footsteps on the street. More voices. I felt the blade slip between my fingers & clatter heavily to the ground. I turned my head in slow motion & saw people coming down the sidewalk. A door opening across the pavement. My grandfather's face.

And then I was running. No-one stood in my way. I ran blindly, guided by some fatal instinct. The car was where I'd left it, behind the wrecker's yard. Long minutes seemed to pass, wiring the ignition until it caught. Mind frantic. Hands gone numb. I drove crazily, fishtailing on gravel, down rutted back roads. Headlights gone dim. Plummeting through the night, tunnel-visioned, rpm in the red, avoiding that face in the rear view mirror.

At any moment I expected something to come out of the dark & put an end to it, like the hand of God. But there was nothing. Only the emptiness. I was driving through it the way you drive through a landscape. A desert. A vast flat open space. I imagined, beyond the headlights, a straight line stretching off to infinity.

♠

The house by the lake was in darkness. I found the gate & the dirt lane leading up to it. It stood out from the pre-dawn like an intuited presence, barely a silhouette. I don't know why I expected her to be there still. Guilt? Desire? Or something else? The ropes were lying tangled on the bed. She'd managed to free herself, take her clothes & run. Everything else was the way I'd left it. I searched around the lake, but there were no signs. I stopped & tried to breathe. It was madness to go on.

I knelt down at the end of the jetty, not knowing why. In the moonlight my hands were dark with blood. There was blood all over me. I stripped-off my jacket & shirt. Plunged my face into the water, stirring up mud. I could feel the cold settling into me, but it seemed remote, like a finger prodding beneath the skin under anaesthesia. I knew this was the end, that I'd fucked-up everything. I should've killed myself right then, while I had the chance, but I didn't. I didn't do anything. I just knelt there, half-naked, like a monkey chained to a post, empty-eyed, staring into the gloom.

Gradually the moon began to sink behind the hills. I could smell the algae in the lake, the mud along the shoreline, the reeds. A sweet smell like a carcass left in the sun to putrefy. The air teemed with insect noises. It was as if an unseen force was closing in. Life in all its viciousness. Death, regeneration, extinction. And as the vapour seethed out of the earth, I thought of Regen, lying in the middle of the vineyard that first night, a mock of moonbeam in her hair, groaning: "I want it." But the image blurred into its opposite. Her hands, tied at the neck, the whites of her eyes, body jerking beneath my weight. And somewhere out in the night she was there. Alone. Running. Afraid. I tore at my face, crying out, hating myself, what I'd become, & still hearing her voice. Again & again. "I want it. I want it." But what had she wanted?

♠

Back in the house I searched through the mess that was left, not knowing what I was looking for. The last time she'd run, she'd gone to the border. But she knew I'd follow her there. And besides, her passport was at the bottom of the suitcase she'd left behind. I turned the pages, all of them still unmarked. Her face smiled up at me. Hair tied back. A white lace collar buttoned at the neck. Her face & beside it a name, a number, a date & place of birth. Could she have gone back there? Could she have gone to the cops, even? I told myself it was impossible. I made myself believe it.

That's when I found it. The photograph of Regen with my father. Taken in that very same room, only years earlier, a lifetime earlier, before the house had been left to rot. The cut-out faces on the walls were there. The metal bedposts. The mosquito netting. They'd called it the Snake House. They'd fucked on that same bed, under that window, with the lake outside. How long ago?

Regen had warned me: "Never trust appearances." But I couldn't help it. That photograph said everything. It said too much. It said almost nothing. I'd wanted to believe, like Hänsel & Gretel, that everything comes good in the end. A fairytale that could become real. But in the story, the children don't end up with blood on their hands, like the blood that was on mine. They bring home the bounty to the hapless, forgiven father, & all's well – they've earned their keep after all – & he gets to grow old & forgetful.

But the father in the picture didn't exist any more. Alive or dead, it made no difference. It'd all come to nothing. The little house in the woods, beside the lake, with its hidden secret. Hänsel & Gretel. The mother hanged. The wicked witch somewhere above the world with her crystal ball, cackling.

I struggled to cast off the spell the photograph had put me under, folding it into my trouser pocket. I looked at the time. It wasn't as late as it'd seemed. My mind raced – there had to still be a chance to put everything right. If I could find Regen. Make her understand that it wasn't me who'd done those things. That it was something else. Something in me. A madness. A poison. Something I'd had to get out.

I bolted from the house just as I was, half-naked, Regen's suitcase in my hand. I turned the car around & drove cross-country towards Prague. A sudden certainty that she'd try to get back there, but not knowing why or how. I drove north & then west, keeping to the main roads this time. Looking for her all along the way. Scanning the roadsides. City-limit truck stops. Petrol stations. Faces of hitchhikers flaring in the headlights.

I saw her everywhere, but found her nowhere. Just outside Prague the car ran out of gas. I grabbed the suitcase & began walking – the lights of Černý Most like a mirage in the distance. At dawn I fell asleep in a ditch, finally overcome. A black sleep in which nothing appeared. When I awoke it was already growing dark. At first I was confused, not knowing whether the day was coming or going. Sixteen hours in sixteen seconds. The air had turned humid. Dark clouds hung on the horizon, moving in from the west. Insects swarmed above the tall grass.

I found a bus stop & rode into the city. No-one paid me any attention. It was a dead run, all the way to Palmovka. When I got to *St Pauli's* there was someone there in the apartment we'd been living in only a couple of days before. But it wasn't Regen. A prostitute from the club was washing herself at the sink. She barely registered me, a stupid doped-out vacancy in her eyes. I searched the room but there was nothing.

Through the open window I could see the dockside all lit up under floodlights. Silhouettes of people walking along the street. I thought I saw Regen there & struggled not to call out. I ran back down the stairs. Drunken voices spilled from the nightclub out onto the sidewalk. I followed the lights along the water to the bridge. A night tram stalled ahead of me, blocking my path. I saw people staring at me through the windows & realised I was standing there still half naked – face & hands smeared with dirt & blood, clutching a battered old suitcase.

Then the sky opened up & the rain came down. Lightly at first, then heavily. I staggered blindly into the headlights, water in my eyes. Fearing I'd lost her for good this time. It began to pour. I could see almost nothing & what I could see didn't seem real. I told myself she wasn't there – that she was a hundred miles away, cringing beside a road somewhere, mad with fear. But halfway across the bridge she was there again, leaning against a concrete railing with the city lights behind her. She was wearing a black coat – the same coat she'd worn the night we left the *Ace of Spades*. It drooped under the weight of the rain soaking it, slipping down. Her hair clung to bare pale shoulders. I lunged at the traffic, trying to get to the other side. Horns blaring. And for a second she stood there almost in front of me, naked, her coat at her feet, high heels teetering. And then she was gone.

# 24
## TRÓJA

It's ten years ago. I'm standing on a bridge in Prague, watching the river haemorrhage into the lower reaches of the city, its turbid waters cascading over the weirs. Black rain drags across the sky. Distant police sirens echo along the quays. Darkness closing in like nightfall across a vast Jurassic swamp.

I'm standing there holding a battered suitcase. In the hot rain I'm shivering & the shivering doesn't stop. The red eye of the TV tower floats above the city. Black shapes rise & fall. I've been standing there for hours, watching the red eye blinking its futile Morse. The rain soaks through me. Wrapped in the darkness of a city that doesn't belong to me.

For the first time I begin to realise I'm utterly alone. I stand there waiting for something to take its course. The shape of Regen's coat lying sodden at the base of the railing & her shoes beside it.

From the other end of the bridge, a pair of blue revolving lights drifts through the rain. A dumb sense of ending comes over me. I'm exhausted, empty. I begin raising my hands, like they do in films. But the revolving lights don't stop. I blink after them. Sheets of water spraying up off the road as a patrol car glides past. I stare after it in confusion. Red taillights receding.

A siren wails across the island. Lights flicker through the trees. I stand there, squinting through heavy slanting rain, arms half-raised in the air like a scarecrow or a lunatic. One of the escaped crazies from Bohnice, waiting to be picked up in the street. Somewhere someone must've made a mistake.

They must be looking for me by now. They'll come back. They won't just leave me like this.

I let my arms drop. Put my hands together, palm-up. Rain water spills over them. Where does all the blood go? These are the same hands I owned when I was a child, only bigger now. A child afraid of the dark, of the man under the bed. How long ago? Regen, holding my hand in the night, guiding me between her thighs, making me forget. Calling me her love.

Was it really her? The streetlight where she was standing before is nothing but a blur. I stare at it. Eyes groping through the rain. But there's no sign. The shape of her coat's gone, her shoes. I can't see them. Down below the river churns. I clutch the railing. Struggle against vertigo. Under my feet, the bridge casts impenetrable shadows, straight down into an abyss. The sound of rain across the water like the swarming of bees.

I turn & keep turning without knowing what else to do. I imagine footsteps. Regen's voice. She's somewhere ahead of me, behind me, on the other side of the bridge. I follow each sound hopelessly. Water sloughs across my feet. The rain's unrelenting. Headlights loom & swerve. I'm standing in the middle of the bridge, clutching Regen's suitcase. It's the only thing left. Then all of a sudden there's a flash & an enormous roar & something hissing up in the sky.

I trudge along the bridge to Libeňský Island. An exit ramp slopes down past an auto bazaar. Orange light flickers across the windscreens of parked cars. Behind the bazaar there's an inlet. A river barge, lying low in the water, is on fire. Flames withering in the rain. A dozen car alarms are screaming in chorus like some apocalyptic symphony falling on deaf ears. I watch the fire die down & then move on. The

159

sound of alarms fading. The rain taking possession of everything.

♠

Time folds back. Six months ago, below decks on the barge tied up at Libeňský Island, listening to Blake talking his talk. The sense of a circle closing. The end returning to the beginning. I'd come back – to the bridge, to the island – in search of ghosts. In the full light of day, everything looked brown, faded, overexposed. I tried to see it as it was in my mind. I kept coming back to the wrecked barge lightning had struck all those years before. An old Greek lived there. He watched me come & go, sizing me up, until one day he made a proposition.

The barge was really just a shell. Everything that'd worked had been ripped out. There was only a cabin, a galley, a shitcan & a pirate cable wired into a fuse box. It suited me like that. The rest of it was sound enough not to fall apart & sink. Back then, that night in the rain, only part of the hold had burned, under the deck plates. The lightning had gouged a hole that'd been welded back over. But the scars still showed.

I began reassembling things the way I remembered them. Bits & pieces. I went to *St Pauli's* & watched the girls, looking for a face. I drank. I walked the streets until they became familiar again. Sometimes, at night, I wondered if there was anyone still out there looking for me. Whoever I was. A dead man on the Amazon. A ghost inside a camera at the bottom of a river.

But no-one ever came. No-one except Blake.

"The truth always catches up with you," my mother used to say. Some people say it's the past that catches up with you. It doesn't matter what you call it – there's always something that'll figure your number out. And when that happens, there's no getting away. Maybe that's why I'd come back. Tired of running. Secretly wanting someone to step out of the shadows & say the game's up.

In La Paz, none of that mattered. Bit by bit I confessed everything. It was the turning point. Blake was the stranger I'd never expected to meet again. He tended my confessions with care. Fed the nightmares that produced them. Sold me my curatives. "Live each day," he said, "as if what you do cancels out the day before."

But nothing ever cancels out anything. I knew that now, watching him sit there across the galley with his camera & half a bottle of booze in front of him. Telling me that everything's part of a machine. That things happen, but *what* happens isn't what matters most. It's the fact they keep on happening, regardless.

"Learn to be like a machine," he tells me, "& you won't have to suffer. Look at the world. It's the only option anyone's got left."

Later we're watching the afternoon settle-in over the river. The fishing line's still hanging slack in the water, beside the green deckchair, where I'd left it. The place seems smaller now that Blake's there. Like another voice in your head that begins as a whisper & gradually crowds you out. He stands at the bow looking down into the shadows of the river, camera slung over his shoulder, its lens pointing back at me.

"You'll never catch anything this way," he says, kicking my line.

"Doesn't matter."

There's a grappling pole lying on the deck beside the line. Blake picks it up. Then without warning he pulls a .38 from his jacket, aims it straight down into the water & fires. The shot echoes through the trees, birds fly up into the air. Even before the echo's died, he thrusts the grappling pole over the edge & heaves it back up with one hand. There's a mutilated carp twitching at the end of it. He drops it at my feet, wrenching the hook free. Blood spatters across my boots. He tosses me the pole, slipping the gun away.

Our eyes meet. "Everything," he says. *"Everything matters."*

♠

Or what matters is that there's always more than just one path to the truth. The truth as it seems to be & the truth yet to come. There's no such thing as original sin, or of any other kind of sin – there's only what a person commits. *It doesn't matter if you know why.* Waiting for the dawn the way you wait for revelation. But dawn reveals only unseen things, not the unknowable. Standing in the shadow of a sky that spreads out like an ocean, & everything that lies beyond it, & everything that doesn't.

Here, in this present time in which I think & am, I tell myself I'm alone. I call out but nobody answers, not even an echo. It must be some kind of dream, this world I pretend each day to inhabit. A world made out of fragments – of things desired, remembered, seen. A whole mirror maze of nonsense. In the fairytale that I am, there's no more Hänsel & Gretel, no evil witch, no mother dead in a tree, no father butchered in his sleep. There are only reflections. All of them unreal.

But the world isn't a dream, & I'm not alone here.

I turn to Inessa & see in her eyes a reflection of all the things I've never been. My lips tremble. I want to tell her how much I hate myself, my history, my cowardice. But they're nothing but words, after all. And words, like the truth, are pliable as wax, to be re-moulded by the barest fraction of a caress.

Below us a whole panorama is emerging from its shadows. We've climbed the steep road up the hillside that looks down over Trója on the city's edge. Does she even know why she's brought me here? Standing on a ruined terrace, a stone balustrade with a stone lion above vineyards sloping down. To one side, the zoo. To the other, the river arcing away towards the east beneath its bridges. The grey shape of the city rises on either side. On this dreary Bohemian coast, we stand & watch the seagulls wheel above the water, swooping & diving.

I wonder if this is what it means to be at peace. Immersed in a scenery to contemplate the big thoughts by. To reach out through your eyes into the soul of the world. Something unbounded, vaster than music, forever beyond our grasp. Like God. Or death. But when I look at that bleak winter of a city, all I really see is a meat grinder giving birth to a bloodied mess.

Inessa stirs beside me. "It always seems bigger than it is," she says.

The river? Prague? The world? Life? All of them perhaps. I follow her gaze down along the quays. A lone figure is riding a motorcycle along the shore road towards the river bend. I picture Blake, hair on end, on his black Enfield, like some Mephistopheles on speed. He'll be waiting for me, I know. But the night's made my decision: there's no going back now. When something's born, you cut the umbilicus. When something dies, you bury it.

♠

I don't know when it began to rain again. It came down lightly, almost like a mist, barely wetting our faces as we

163

looked at one another & then up at the sky. I reached out with my arm & held Inessa closer to me.

"You're right," I said, not sure any longer what it was she was right about, but whatever it was I felt we must be in agreement, in concord.

And so we stood there in the rain in Trója, on the ruined terrace looking out over the small fenced-in vineyard. The centuries-old vineyard that'd survived it all – occupation, war, communism. A miracle. Or a madness.

A group of gypsy children were shouting at one another from a yard nearby, their voices blown about on the breeze. Someone was hanging laundry on a balcony in the greyblue project down in the valley. A tram rattled over the rail bridge above the weir.

At the river bend, the long narrow fingers of the docklands stretched out of the early morning haze. Beyond, a vista of tenements & tower blocks spread across the horizon. We looked down at the grape vines clinging to the earth so tenuously, & wondered what they were doing there.